WITHDRAWN

The Marriage
of Saints

American Indian Literature and Critical Studies Series
Gerald Vizenor, General Editor

The Marriage
of Saints

A Novel

DAWN KARIMA PETTIGREW

University of Oklahoma Press : Norman

Library of Congress Cataloging-in-Publication Data

Pettigrew, Dawn Karima.
   The marriage of saints : a novel / Dawn Karima Pettigrew.
      p.   cm. — (American Indian literature and critical studies
   series ; v. 52)
   ISBN 0-8061-3787-8 (hc : alk. paper)
   1. Reservation Indians—Southern States—Fiction.
2. Cherokee Indians—Southern States—Fiction. 3. Creek
Indians—Southern States—Fiction. 4. Marriage—Fiction.
5. Indian reservations—Southern States—Fiction. I. Title.
II. Series.
   PS3616.E88M37 2006
   813'.6—dc22   2006040486

The Marriage of Saints: A Novel is Volume 52 in the American
Literature and Critical Studies Series.

The paper in this book meets the guidelines for permanence
and durability of the Committee on Production Guildelines for
Book Longevity of the Council on Library Resources, Inc. ∞

1 2 3 4 5 6 7 8 9 10

For my parents. I love you, I thank you,
and I thank God for you.

The Marriage
of Saints

The Pursuit of Darkness

Indiana Redpaint Telling

I will never eat another fish. I owe fish a debt and I plan to pay. Trout, bass—none of them have anything to fear from me. So you want to hear a fish story, that takes a little bit of doing.

Some men have wealth. Others own land. Jack StandsStraight, my daddy, had Tennessee Jane. Tennessee Jane came along at the end of the middle, where it is hard enough to be noticed, let alone be first at much of anything. Even though God left her between my big sisters and myself, He blessed her with a spectacular kind of beauty. Young men dreamed dreams and old men hid and watched until Tennessee Jane grew up.

Tennessee Jane was useless. She never could cook, refused to learn. She sat in the scrubgrass yard of Daddy's little house, watching for a seam to burst in the sky. Daddy let her alone, since daydreaming looks a lot like virtue, and virtue in girls like Tennessee Jane is just the thing that makes bankers, doctors, even Hollywood come calling with blankets and cash money. My sister's smile on fire from Heaven, stirred in with her tendency to chase after Jesus, were better for Daddy than an old-age retirement policy.

Me, I make things happen. It rains when I pray, thunders when I tantrum. I dream that I stumble over a bushel basket of rattlesnakes, then rebuke them just to see what will happen. My cool hands cross broken bodies, reclaim hurt limbs from odd angles, pressing them into another day of service.

People talk like life is solid, but it's not. Life moves like clear water, only harder to catch. There are moments when we dam it up, send it streaming a different way, and then marvel when the water falls into other folks' lives. That's how I see it. About half the time, a body isn't living just their own life, but swimming in somebody else's spillover.

How Tennessee Jane ended up hurt by that GoingBack boy is just like that. Daddy sent me everywhere with my older sister, made me watch over her. Keep her pure, he said, don't let her scratch her long legs on rocks or mar her pretty face. Entertain her so she don't look out too far toward the world or take up with strangers. So, you can imagine me, tearing through the woods, screaming for my sister, who was carried off by the GoingBack boy, the middle one, not even the oldest, who had gone to the service and learned a trade, but the middle boy, who as near as I could figure, had a way with cars, but couldn't write his own name.

Daddy searched, took all nine of his brothers with him. Drove all night and never did find her.

"You lost me my future," Daddy said squarely. He stared into the round eyes of eggs my sister Georgia fried. "If you want a place to stay other than the road, you go get it back."

Now you can judge me if you want. It's easy to convict a body of all kinds of things. What I did might not have been all right, but you tell me, if you had been fourteen and not much to look at, wouldn't you have done pretty much the same thing?

Wore my shoes out searching. Wrapped my feet in warm ashes and cotton and kept on. The rising of the sun and its setting came and went seventeen times, as I walked. Didn't find her.

Funny how most of your prayers get answered on the way home. Following the river back towards our home-place, I noticed a ribbon of blood in the water. I ran against the river, upstream and into my sister. Well, into what was left of her.

Tennessee Jane's sweet face was swollen with water. Bruises inked the outlines of her eyes. I pressed my hands against her torn fingers, matching every inch of her body with one of mine.

"Please don't be dead," I begged. "Please, please, please." My tears watered my sister's eyes. I whispered every name I could remember for God.

Tennessee Jane whimpered. I rejoiced. That is, until I looked up and there was Darrell Earl GoingBack sitting on the far side of the bank. Fishing.

It is something what a body can do mad. My sister's broken body felt like a sack of goosedown on my back. I would carry her home, away from hands that shatter bone. As I turned, there was Darrell Earl GoingBack, fishing away, like he hadn't wronged Tennessee Jane one bit.

"Someday, Darrell Earl GoingBack," I whispered, "you will catch a fish that will talk to you."

The rest of it, I heard this way. Darrell Earl caught a fish that day. Swam right alongside him and jumped up onto the shore, clear into the bucket.

"I don't want to catch you," Darrell Earl said.

"Well, you did," replied the fish, just as natural as if fish are prone to talking all the time.

So Darrell Earl picked him up, going against everything in his natural mind. Stopped by his mama's house and asked her to clean his catch.

"No, sir." There went that fish chit-chatting again, scaring Darrell Earl's mama something awful. "You caught me, now you clean me."

Darrell Earl's hands moved themselves. Scales and bones spread blood across his no-account fingers and onto the floor. Darrell Earl asked his mama, who couldn't hardly move for horror, to cook the fish for him.

"Excuse me, but no." There went that fish speaking out again. "You cleaned me, now you cook me."

Darrell Earl's mama to this day claims she can't forget the pain on her son's face. He floured and fried that fish. She said it was as if he was watching his own self work, not wanting to, but still doing it.

"Mama!" Darrell Earl cried out, realizing that this fish wasn't no ordinary one. "Mama, come eat this fish with me!" Like that would keep him from getting what was coming to him.

Darrell Earl's mama didn't budge. The fish cleared its throat and sighed.

"No," it explained, "You know you cooked me. You have to eat me."

Darrell Earl choked on the second bite. Fell down dead as dead gets right in the middle of his mama's linoleum.

They put him in the ground Tuesday evening. Tennessee Jane woke Wednesday morning with the face of an angel. Married a Holiness preacher, took off circuit riding. I came up on the rough side of the mountain. I stay out of folks' way. I never go fishing.

You asked for a fish story. There it is. Things have a way of working out one way or the other. Life is like that. You do right, or catch the fish that you deserve.

Mourner's Bench

Carolina StandsStraight Speaking

You don't have to tell everything you know. You don't have to and can't nobody make you. That's what Daddy always said, when we went up to sign our names at the rodeo. I say sign lightly, since Daddy never could read or write much that I ever saw. He made an X, big as day where the name was supposed to go. He made a big show out of the fact that he could make straight lines with either hand.

"Comes from being hurt more than a time or two," he'd say, meaning how he'd been bumped and bruised more than a little bit. One thing though, neither me or Daddy has ever broken a bone. Ever. Never ever. Daddy was proud as he could be about that and he wasn't shy about saying so to anybody who'd listen, which was about everybody. Daddy was movie-show handsome, with a split in his chin and everything. If he'd been white, he'd have been in pictures.

Somebody asked him once. A studio, looking for Indians to come out to Hollywood, Burbank really, and ride horses and holler in movies. Daddy, being a cowboy all his life, was a natural. A natural. Funny how people say that, like sitting on a wild pony is just something you do from the womb. Only maybe it is. I mean, it was for me.

The first thing I remember is horses. Now I know what people say, how you can't remember being born or much before your first, most likely second, birthday. Like how they say babies don't know enough to smile. Way I see it, people underestimate babies. You want to know who to leave your wallet with? Watch babies. If a baby don't like them, you don't either. Just walk away.

Same thing with places. Ever been somewhere and had this uneasy feeling, like something evil might of made its way in there too, and next thing you know, a baby goes to hollering? Uh-huh. That's what I'm talking about. Went over to a funeral for rodeo clown, Theo Jones, a Black Seminole from over in Lawton. He married a girl over there, or something. Never did know her, but I'll tell you true, Old Theo must have loved her. I mean, he never did mess around on her, and he had plenty of chances. He went to sleep every night exactly one-half hour after the rodeo ended, after he took him a bath and ate a cheese sandwich and jam. Strawberry jam, right out of the jar. Had him a spoonful or two, and went right to sleep. Daddy asked him why he did that once, and he said it tasted just like his wife. Just like that. Well, that set well with Daddy, on account of he would carry the world if Mama asked him to.

Anyhow, Old Theo passed on, old as old gets, leaving his wife with about every penny he ever earned doing anything he ever did. Me and Daddy went over to the funeral in Lawton, and if I ever saw anything packed out like that before or since, I don't know it. Little bitty church, with clapboard walls and one of those paintings of Jesus that looks like He never did a lick of work in His life, which we know He did, and hard work, too. When I got saved, I know I got me a Savior that could stand to stay out in the sun, and didn't have no problem whipping the fire out of the devil. So Daddy and I make our way around the folks standing every place they could put their feet inside and outside.

"Just like Heaven," Daddy says. He intends to whisper, but quiet isn't his strong point. I can't for the life of me think of what he means. Last I heard of it, Heaven wasn't nothing like a hot box of a church, where folks was sweating and shifting their weight from foot to foot and setting anywhere their behinds would fit.

"It is too like Heaven," Daddy says again. Me and Daddy, we always did know what the other was thinking, right at the moment the other was thinking it. Mama claimed Daddy would have carried me for nine months if he could have found a way, but since he couldn't, he made up for it by carrying me everywhere he could. In his arms until I got too big, then on his horse or in his truck with him. That's what made us think the same thoughts, since we saw all the same things every day of the world.

"All colors, all kinds," Daddy says, and then I can see it. "Everybody will be welcome and they'll have plenty of places to sit."

You recall what I was saying about babies? Well, there's this sugarlump right in front of me, not more than a few months old, eyes wide open and looking at everything. All of the sudden, a big man walks in, pretty good sized, with hair I think is white, until I realize it's the color of cornsilk. I don't put two and two together until the baby starts hollering.

Just hollering, like you pinched it, which it was so sweet you'd never do. The mama tries to calm it, then Daddy tries, and I never did know a baby or a person that was right in the head that didn't care for Daddy. People keep singing "Pass Me Not" over top of the screaming, and then that blond man just up and leaves. Baby quits, just like that.

Years later, that man with the cornsilk hair beat his wife so bad her own mama couldn't recognize her when she went to pick out her body at the morgue. So you see, babies know. And all that talk about smiling just being gas or colic, that's hogwash. Babies know how to smile when they want to. They know who they like and they know who they don't want no truck with. And they remember.

I do. I remember horses. You know how most people, when they go in a stable, their faces tear up from the smell? Well, I'm the other way round. That smell I know, it's what feels familiar. It's when I wash up and go in Mama's house that the smells of family and food and people startle me. I have to get accustomed to it all over again.

When I was little, I used to bring hay into the house. Put clean straw under my pillow. Mama moved it on account of I slept with my sister Georgia, who sneezed. Once the house went silent and Daddy started making sleeping noises, I'd sneak out to the barn and sleep in the middle of clean hay. Frost came without warning one night and I about froze. Mama made me a tiny pillow out of gingham and filled it with hay. She left a corner undone so I could put fresh hay in it anytime I got the inclination. I still carry that pillow. I don't believe in luck, but I've worn it in more than a few rodeos.

I was born on a horse. Mama was just little then herself. Daddy had went out to Cherokee, North Carolina, with his first cousin Wayman to the Swain County Baptist and Holiness revival. They held it every three years, to show there was no ill will held by the Baptists who lost their kinfolk to the tongue talkers. Cousin Wayman talked Daddy into helping him drive out there. Said the girls out there were pretty as flowers. Plus most everybody they knew out here was kin. Which is true of there same as here, if you think about it. After all, we used to live in the mountains of North Carolina until the Trail of Tears walked us from there to Oklahoma. So we're all family, one way or another. But Daddy and Cousin Wayman didn't take no time for a history lesson. I guess they reckoned on seeing pretty girls their mamas didn't know.

The first Sunday morning, sometime between the offering and the altar call, Cousin Wayman got the call to preach and Daddy fell in love. Mama was praying fervently, probably for lost sinners, which Daddy had spent the past eighteen years proving he was and Cousin Wayman had just been. Just like that, Daddy stepped out into the aisle and went to the altar.

"Save me, Jesus," he hollered. Daddy never was one to do anything on the downlow. The pastor started praying and the congregation shouted. When Daddy lifted his head, the first thing he saw was Mama. Her head was bowed and she was praying, her lips just going, even after the pastor said, "Amen."

Daddy knew two things: he had made it into Heaven by the skin of his teeth and he had found himself a wife. A few minutes, and an introduction later, Daddy was sure of two certainties in life—eternal security and 'til death do them part.

"When I found me a girl named Oklahoma in North Carolina, I knew it must be some kind of sign, especially when she called me foolish, right to my face, for thinking so."

I never did see how being called foolish was a sign of true love.

Daddy explained. "She risked hellfire and damnation to tell me what she thought. She must have cared something about me."

They married right there at Wright's Creek Baptist Church. I never did know what Daddy did to get Mama past thinking he was born foolish and into saying, "I do." Don't matter to me, I guess. Whatever he did, I was born exactly nine months to the day after their wedding. The exact day after. Not a day before, or a day before the day before. On a horse. Horses troubled Mama, but Daddy had got her up on one named Cleo. Just standing still, when all of a sudden Mama cried out. Blood and water soaked the saddle and blanket. Daddy reached up for her and there I was. My head anyway. The rest of me was born on a pile of hay.

"The horses got so quiet," Daddy told me. "Usually, horses, they don't kindly like blood, but that day they just stood there. Never moved a muscle. Didn't even seem to mind you bloodying their dinner."

Daddy cut the cord with his knife. He picked up Mama and me and started toward the house. Right about then, Cleo started whinnying and stomping her foot.

"She wanted to see you," Daddy said, "Wouldn't stop making a fuss until I brought you up close to her face. She sniffed at you. Threw a fit every day until I brought you out to see her. Wasn't long after that, I started wrapping you in a blanket and putting you on the saddle. Cleo walked so slow, you didn't even wake up."

I rode Cleo almost every day of my life. Her tombstone is next to Daddy's stable.

So that's what I mean when I say maybe me riding horses does come natural. But as for the rest of it, I'm not so sure I can tell you what you want to know.

Nobody ever tells their whole testimony. They tell just enough to sound like they needed saving and no more. The rest of it, if they told it, might make you wonder if they really were saved enough to eat with the rest of us. That's why I'm telling you, the best I know how.

I was not there when it happened. I stayed home with Mama on account of it was planting time. She needed me to break up the ground for her. If I'd gone, I think now, if I'd only gone, maybe none of us would be the way we are now.

But I didn't go. Daddy went by himself. Signed my youngest sister away in exchange for the entry fees. Came in second, came home talking about how he'd promised Indiana to a steer wrestler as collateral. The day before he came to claim her, Indiana fell down a well. Not the main one, but the old one on the back end of our property. Mama came running to tell me. We filled that well with dirt, and the preacher came and said a few words over it.

Daddy got bad to drink after that. Tennessee married that preacher, so there was only Georgia left at the house. Me, I stayed gone at the rodeo.

My grandmama used to say the story is all in how the storyteller tells it. I reckon that's right. I reckon we're all right in our own ways, and we pay for our wrongs in our own ways, too.

The Boiling Point of Conquest

Jack StandsStraight Measuring Sugar and Blood

First thing you do, you offer the fork,
Shake hands with silver and trade him for tools,
Before the chief makes you for some kind of fool,
Pick up your spoon and show him how to use it.

Chime fork tines against the rim of a plate,
Rounder and whiter than baked clay or baskets
And better for catching the runoff of grease,
Which you'll get to later, somewhere behind flour,
Salt, white sugar, lard, and fat meat.

Next, don't neglect to give him the cup.
He'll need something to wash death down,
Carry oil to arteries, flush fat, wither muscles,
Which once outrode, outwarred your guns.

Offer him spirits in place of his soul,
So he'll agree to the exchange rate in Hell,
Fire for water, and ashes for dust,
He'll behave as he must to keep the drinks flowing.

Finally, finish and make you a country,
Built on the breaking of bread and bones.
Make bricks of pork and gates of foam,
Until eating begins to claim your own.

None of This Could I Have Known

Nathan Hollow Stealing

Nathan Hollow delivers ice. He drives across the reservation, only there is no such thing as across the reservation. It is more like above and below, the tires rolling into and out of the pockmarked roads.

Georgia StandsStraight hangs the wash. She wrings each piece of cotton one last time before hanging it between weathered wooden clothespins. The garments release water in uneven streams onto the grass below the taut line. Drops splatter the dry earth and her ankles. Something about her feet, broad and vulnerable in the tall grass and wet dirt, moves Nathan Hollow. His breath catches somewhere between his throat and the back of his tongue. A sudden smoke burns his nostrils. For a moment the leaves fall, one after another from the trees.

"Hey!" Nathan Hollow calls out, as much to stop the vision of trees burning as anything else. He has no business calling her, this Baptist girl, whose mother can talk directly to God. Nathan Hollow's grandmother, who conducts imaginary music from her narrow bed at the Vinita Convalescent Home, used to stop in the middle of sentences and reply to the Almighty. God gave her grocery lists and shoe sizes. He might just tell Oklahoma

StandsStraight that Nathan Hollow is messing with her little girl.

"Hey," he calls again. Can a man take fire in his bosom and not get burned? He hears Nanny say that, only she says burnt. Burnt. Flame and cinders. Nathan Hollow delivers ice. He knows what heat means.

"Come here," he calls. She does, which startles him. Her eyes are empty. Clear. Clean. He should let her alone. "You hot?"

Georgia StandsStraight nods. Nathan Hollow leans out of the window of the Clarity Ice Company truck. "Meet me around back."

Georgia StandsStraight shakes her wet hands as she heads toward the back of the truck. Nathan Hollow follows her round form, made of circle set upon circle. Even her hair spirals into a hairpinned bun over the orb of her plump neck.

As Nathan Hollow raises the door, cool air swirls against the scorch of summer. Georgia StandsStraight leans forward into the chill, and in that moment, Nathan Hollow pushes her. He will never be able to explain how his burly arms moved against her ample bottom, but the memory of his hands pressing upward against her thighs will ride shotgun with him until he ends his life with a razor. The accordion folds of the truck door fall shut, silencing Georgia StandsStraight's screams.

Heat from Georgia's body melts the sack of ice beneath her. Blood and water pool on the cool floor. Sweat trickles down Nathan Hollow's back and sides, reminding him of a strange kind of fire.

"I don't want my wife knowing nothing about this," Nathan Hollow whispers. His hands tighten around Georgia StandsStraight's wrists. Under the flesh, the bones protrude, sharp and accusatory. She blinks at him.

Nathan Hollow tosses her roundness and two bags of ice into the grass below. As he drives away, Nathan Hollow sees Georgia Standstraight sobbing behind him, her body curled into a perfectly round *O*.

Witty Inventions

Georgia StandsStraight Smith Finding

This is what I do. First, I take a bath, in water so hot it scalds. Second, right after that night's prayer meeting, I drink long and deep from the cold water fountain. Third, I kiss Colton Smith. He was in love with my sister, Tennessee Jane. My cold tongue chases the warmth from his lips. Colton settles for me. Seven weeks later, he marries me at Talequah Baptist. Five months later, we quarrel over him driving out of Talequah in the snow. He cannot understand why I am all the time so cold.

No Child Until

Elisabeth Hollow Noticing

I stand in the middle of the cashier's aisle at the grocery. I hold two ten-dollar bills as if they were rubies washed up by the river. That is like my husband, Nathan, afraid of keeping Andrew Jackson in a pocket too close to his heart. Then, I see Oklahoma StandsStraight, beautiful as the next world, laying a ten-dollar bill on the counter in exchange for ice. That girl of Georgia's, the one Colton Smith claims, rides all wrapped up on Oklahoma's back. The blanket hides her face for a moment. When she lifts her tiny head, her cold eyes and pale face show me there are no words for what I know.

The Boundary of Moab

Deuteronomy 24:19

GEORGIA STANDSSTRAIGHT SMITH
WIDOWED BY SNOW

Sorrow at dawn, again at dusk,
Grinds our insides, knots our bellies,
Pangs fingerwoven from the remembrance of meat.
Our cheeks draw close together, water, sour with dry
    flour.

Some mornings, I wake weeping,
Fold my soul within my hand,
Press my will into my lips.
With each tear, I covet the salt of Lot's wife.

Half an omer of joy would buy our lives.
We survive on the crumbs field bosses disdain,
Pray they are clumsy, leave handfuls behind.
What they esteem lightly enlightens our eyes.

Nights make us ache for when we had peace,
Were people of plenty, had more than we needed.
There were grapes in that land it took two to carry.
Of course, there were not.

That was Canaan.
We know it.
Memory satisfies one kind of hunger.

Shewbread

Georgia StandsStraight Smith Flying

Georgia's eye hurts like the Tribulation. Indigo seeps into her eyelid, shadows the socket with creeping pain. Throbbing is next. Four horsemen and their brothers ride roughshod over Georgia's injured eye, stopping only to strike the bridge of her nose. "We must go away from here," she tells her daughter. And maybe because the man she stayed with hates Elvis, or maybe because *Frankie and Johnny* was on last night, Georgia takes the baby and their money, some egg salad and grape jelly, flags down the Greyhound and rides to Graceland.

Georgia and her daughter know how to wait. The woman behind them in the line to see Graceland does not. She sighs repeatedly and shuffles her canvas mules. The chain smokers standing two lives in front of Georgia notice her ink-blue eye and then ignore her. She is nothing to them. They turn their heads, iced with blue frosting, and debate Elvis' death.

"Now you know he is too dead," the first woman wrinkles her mouth to say. "Would Graceland have all us standin' on our feet like this if he wasn't really in the ground?"

The second woman clicks her tongue between her dentures and the roof of her mouth.

"You never know. Alls it is I'm saying is that it seems mighty peculiar to me, him having that dead twin and all. Mighty convenient. Exactly how I'd hide, if I wanted to shy away from the fans and all."

"But what about Priscilla and Lisa Marie?" The first woman shifts her "I-heart-bingo" tote bag from one shoulder to the other. "And his mama? You think Elvis, who was surely raised right, would do a thing like up and vanish and dishonor his mama?"

The second woman shakes her head slowly.

"Well, he was raised better than that, I suppose."

Both women look at Georgia, suddenly. The first woman calls over the shoulders of the people between them.

"Are you Indian, Sugar? You know, Elvis Presley was part Indian."

Georgia thought that when she saw *Jailhouse Rock*. "I'm Cherokee."

"Just like Elvis, what did I tell you?" The first woman lights another cigarette and looks over her bifocals at her companion.

Georgia thinks that Elvis is probably Choctaw. She starts to say so, but the line moves. The wait to see Graceland is over. So is the discussion.

Georgia and her daughter share a carton of orange juice. Georgia has just enough money for a hot dog. They sit in the shadow of too much money and take small bites to make their meal last longer. Georgia regrets that they have no souvenirs, but believes that the baby needs food more than a Love Me Tender T-shirt, which she will outgrow in a season anyway. Her daughter swallows the last of the fruit juice and burps. Georgia pats her back.

A dog, spotted with brown and white, strolls up to Georgia. He sits at her feet, smiling at her, showing every pointed tooth in his head.

"I'm sorry, dog," Georgia says. She waves politely. The dog wags his tail. "I already put ketchup on this. You won't like it."

The dog begs prettily. His spots remind Georgia of freckles. She relents. It will be good for her daughter to see that, even poor, they remember how to give.

"Here," Georgia hands over her dinner. The dog takes the hot dog and bounds away.

"Howdy, Ma'am." A stranger strides up to Georgia. He is tall, and the freckled dog runs up next to his blue suede shoes.

"Ma'am," the stranger says, offering his right hand to Georgia. She wipes her palm on a napkin before she takes it. The sunshine sends rainbows through his enormous diamond ring.

"Ma'am," the stranger continues, "I'd sure like to thank you for feeding my hound dog."

The stranger squeezes Georgia's fingers and moves away. The dog follows, looking back once to smile. Georgia lifts her daughter's tiny left hand, and makes it wave. When Georgia opens her own right hand, there is a fifty in her palm.

Georgia's man is coming. The clerk at the EZSLEEP motel says this slowly, looking as if he might cry. Georgia's man is coming. The man who took them in when Georgia's husband wrecked and passed away has found them. He called to say that he is on his way. The Greyhound driver told him where they were going. Do not run, Georgia's man says, this will only make things worse. The clerk's bottom lip quivers as he quotes this. The clerk is a gray and quiet man, the color of sheetrock, who orders two orders of chicken chow mein each night and says, "Oh, I guess my eyes are bigger than my stomach," as he gives the second one to Georgia and the baby. He will not take their fifty, says they are helping the motel's image, by making it look like a place for families instead of "riff-raff." Georgia imagines her man's thick fist smashing into the sheetrock clerk.

"No," whispers Georgia to the clerk, whose eyes pool with cloudy tears. "We cannot stay here. Thank you for being so kind. We must be going now."

The clerk covers his eyes with his pale hands and sobs. Wandering away from the EZSLEEP motel's mostly clean bedspreads and tepid bathwater, Georgia fears the man that took her in. As she spreads her jacket on the waste-land that borders the highway, Georgia remembers Colton Smith's pickup, crushed up over ice and under snow. Georgia imagines this man's truck, twisted into garlands of flame.

She puts her daughter on the jacket and covers her with most of their clothes. Kneeling next to her, Georgia winces. Gravel, ground glass, and weeds scrape her knees. She prays in time with the traffic, distracting herself with the sound of her pleading.

"Save us, Lord," Georgia cries. "Stop him. Don't let him find us. Do something . . . *please* . . . "

Her voice sounds plaintive against the rumble of eighteen-wheelers and RVs.

"Amen," Georgia ends. The baby makes a small sound, like doves moaning. When Georgia lifts her eyes, the plains of the moon look almost like home.

Cast Salt

Brother Cousin Wallace Summoned

Prophets owe no debt to sleep.
Before you wed one, you should have known this.
Now you're surprised by the scratch of shouting,
Long before daybreak, as dreams meet spirit.

The measure of rest is a cruel transaction.

We understand and soothe you,
But God has things to do.
Chronicle our lives, our tribes, by streetlight,
Streaming through windows, across the page
Of the parchment we keep by the bed,
For such a time as this.

Seers often rhyme in Braille,
Our fingers warring against lines that seem straight.
Dawn shows them crooked as sticks in water.

We shout by candles you wound last summer,
Useless in any dark but this.
Constellations teach us to number our days.

On the nights when we must testify,
Every watt matters.
All the lamps are impressed into service.
Those sermons, those times,
We light fires.
You roll over,
Anointed to sleep through meter.

A Bed in Hell

Brother Cousin Wallace Finding

Brother Cousin Wallace jerks awake in the feather bed. His wife, Eloise, snores, a light rattle hidden in the bridge of her nose. Throughout the fifty-one years of their marriage, Eloise has learned to sleep through his fitful nights. This was not always so.

At first, when Brother Cousin Wallace would pace their ramshackle house, praying from somewhere deep in his belly, Eloise would bury her head under feather pillows and dove-in-the-window quilts. Deep sleep found her that way once, tangled and covered, and pushed a feather into her open mouth. She inhaled, nearly choked on feathery spines and cotton. Since then, she sleeps above the covers and breathes through her nostrils. Brother Cousin Wallace's night rambling seems not to trouble her at all.

Brother Cousin Wallace wanders out the back door. He paces over the sparse grass and gravel. His bare feet sense nothing under leathery soles and diabetes.

Brother Cousin Wallace is a preacher. This is like saying that red is a color, it is such a matter of local fact. He is sixteen years old, walking behind his daddy's plow, when he hears the rumble of thunder. In that thunder is a voice that sounds like river water or rain.

"Say on, Sir," answers Brother Cousin Wallace, who is nothing if not polite. He is a good boy, prone to moonshine and penny candy, but other than that, hardworking and mannerly. The voice says simply that Brother Cousin Wallace needs to tell people that God is for them and not against them. Not one to contradict, Brother Cousin Wallace nods amiably and sets out to inform The Good Lord about a certain point.

Brother Cousin Wallace cannot read. The alphabet, road signs, billboards, schoolbooks, and hymnals, all cartwheel and rearrange like the stained-glass slivers in a kaleidoscope. Farmwork swallowed schooling when he was twelve. The humiliation of attempting to understand sticks and circles was no great loss to Brother Cousin Wallace.

"Sir, I think You might have the wrong fellow—" Brother Cousin Wallace begins. This is the last thing he remembers. When he comes to himself, he is stretched out on the same ground he walks now, worn-out like he's been in a struggle. Brother Cousin Wallace sits up and dusts himself off. Nothing has changed that he knows of, until he joins his mama and her sister Lucille at the settin'-up for his great-uncle's wife, Mamie. The preacher from the Freewill Baptist Church has been detained and the pastor from the Sovereign Grace Baptist Church has just finished his sermon on a woman named Rizpah, who sat through the turn of the seasons, guarding her dead sons.

Two deaconnesses, Anna Wilson and Mary Landers, get up and sing about Heaven. Then they sing about how roses never fade. Everybody cries. Brother Cousin Wallace stuns himself by walking right up to the pulpit.

"Brethren and Sistern," Brother Cousin Wallace booms, in a voice that even he himself cannot recall hearing. He turns his head toward the Lord's Supper Table, where an oversized King James Bible stays open to the twenty-second chapter of Saint Luke's Gospel. Brother Cousin Wallace should not know this. The fact that he does startles him.

Quickly, he shifts his pale eyes toward a bulletin board that notes the number of students in Sunday School, the number of chapters read, and the amount of the offering. The letters, the numbers mix and twist into an illegible jumble. Brother Cousin Wallace returns his gaze to the written-in-red passages of the Bible's thin pages. "This is my body which is given for you: this do in remembrance of Me," reads the crimson text. Brother Cousin Wallace can read. His amazement manifests in a full-bodied shout, which all the Missionary Baptists take as a sign of Holy Ghost regeneration. Brother Cousin Wallace gets baptized and licensed in the same afternoon.

Brother Cousin Wallace reads nothing but the Bible. He announces this with great satisfaction, to anyone who will stop long enough to listen. That he can only read the King James 1611 version of the Bible serves as proof to him and to others of his singular calling. Newspapers, other versions of the Bible, and farm reports remain garbled, yet Brother Cousin Wallace reads through the minor prophets weekly. He is especially fond of Nahum, who seems to summarize the trouble with the nation, today's young people, and Hollywood in a reasonable amount of space.

While Jesus Christ Himself commands His disciples to "go ye into all the world and preach the Gospel to every creature," Brother Cousin Wallace rarely has enough gasoline to get farther than the next county. For his intents and purposes, Brother Cousin Wallace decides all the world means Cast Salt, Kentucky. This is a sufficient mission field, Brother Cousin Wallace reasons, since it takes a day and an afternoon to cover on foot.

After all, these are his kin. Cousin is his given name, the reward for being related to nearly every soul in Cast Salt, Kentucky, and the neighboring township. The thought of close kin sweltering in eternal damnation settles it. When every soul in Cast Salt is saved from the perils of Hell and other denominations, Brother Cousin Wallace will turn to other towns.

Tonight, Brother Cousin Wallace awakens suddenly. This is not unusual, except that Brother Cousin Wallace struggles to pray through. He tries, repeatedly, to seek God, to find Him in the middle of memorized Scriptures and remembered sermons. Finally, he stumbles out-of-doors.

"Say on, Sir," Brother Cousin Wallace pleads. He turns his head in Heaven's general direction. His neck creaks with the wear and tear of looking up. The moon, full and luminous, fills the night sky. Brother Cousin Wallace watches the sky through irises glazed with the first blues of cataracts.

The stars are going out.

Brother Cousin Wallace gasps. He throws his hands upward. Gnarled fingers grasp at the constellations, as if to keep them lit a while longer.

"Lord, save us!" Brother Cousin Wallace hollers long and loud before realizing he has not made a sound.

The keys are in Brother Cousin Wallace's maroon truck. It is not his, not really, only three-quarters his, just fourteen more payments shy of the title deed. A year and two months, or a year all by itself if he has a good Christmas, and Brother Cousin Wallace will own this truck. Free and clear. There is a sermon in that, Brother Cousin Wallace thinks. For Brother Cousin Wallace, life itself is the best tract.

Cast Salt's farms yield to open spaces and hills. Brother Cousin Wallace crosses the Tennessee state line somewhere between the last line of Hosea and the first sentence of Joel. He chants the prophets from memory, until he reaches Zechariah, the eighth chapter, at the end of the twenty-third verse.

"We will go with you: for we have heard that God is with you."

Brother Cousin Wallace skids into a stop by the roadside. Just right of the breakdown lane, a pile of skirts and blouses fills a spot beside the highway. His brow furrows, as he overturns the garments. Brother Cousin Wallace inhales sharply. Under the outfits, a woman lies still. Cradled in her arms, a baby is blinking at him.

"Lord, have mercy," Brother Cousin Wallace moans. "Who are you, Little Bit? Are you why the sky's falling?"

The baby blinks again. Brother Cousin Wallace stoops, his left knee popping like corn in sizzling oil. He reaches for the baby, trying to pry her from the woman's arms. Brother Cousin Wallace touches the tanned flesh, which is cool underneath his callused palm.

Brother Cousin Wallace considers going for help. He could get the highway patrol, who would investigate the situation. Only they might put the baby in foster care, where there would be no guarantee of a Baptist upbringing. Brother Cousin Wallace is not sure about transporting found infants over state lines, and Eloise is not all the way up to walking the floors at night, what with her having asthma and all. He is weighing the issues and waiting for God to answer, when the baby's eyes begin to close.

"Come back," he shouts, "in the Name of Jesus Christ, come back!"

The woman opens her eyes first. They are round and shadowed with dark lashes. The baby yawns. Brother Cousin Wallace steps backward. God has knocked the wind out of him.

"Much obliged, Lord," he whispers. He bends over, and lifts the pair into the cab of his truck. His strength surprises him. Brother Cousin Wallace drapes his own flannel shirt around the woman and her baby. He climbs in beside them and U-turns back toward Kentucky.

Brother Cousin Wallace glances at his passengers. The woman sleeps deeply. So does the baby. Brother Cousin Wallace gazes at the sky. For the first time in hours, it looks just fine.

Judah Surprised

Brother Cousin Wallace Planning

Near as I reckon it, The Good Lord's always got a plan. The Lord giveth and the Lord taketh away, that's how everybody tends to put it, but the truth is, it's much more the Lord's nature to be giving than to taking.

That's how I see these happenings last night. I take off driving and don't hardly know where I'm headed, just that I need to find whatever, whoever. Really, it is wreaking havoc in the sky, and there's these two in need of help. I make good time there and better time back—so good, if I told you, you'd want to call me a liar. You might not aloud, on account of I'm a preacher, but you'd sure enough think about it, which is sin in itself.

She sleeps through the whole way home. They both do, come to think about it, which is why I have plenty of time to think. Zechariah eight and twenty-three comes up in my soul more times than I can count, each time strong-arming the time before.

I keep thinking about where to put them. They could come home with me, but it wouldn't be too long before Eloise's hard breathing and heart trouble would get the best of her. Of course, I'm foolish to be leaning to my own understanding of this thing anyway, when all a body needs do is inquire of The Good Lord. So I ask Him.

"Lord," I say, "Sir, I surely do thank You for saving these two young folks, especially on account of I don't really know if their souls were headed out into everlasting damnation. I appreciate You, Lord."

I do, too. I don't hardly know what I'm going to do with these two live bodies, much less what I would've done if they'd have been dead.

"Now, Sir, I reckon they've some kind of clout with You. I mean, I'm not altogether sure if anybody but me seen what You did in the sky tonight. But I reckon if You'd wake up a preacher in Kentucky to come out and see about these two in Tennessee, You'd have to care a whole lot about them. Which, plainly, You do, seeing as You saved their lives and such like."

I'm so glad to see Clancy Bailey's place, I don't know what to do. Not too far from Cast Salt. Home. I can't tell you where I've been, on account of I don't read nothing but the Bible—Authorized King James Version, 1611—not even road markers, but I know I've been a ways from home tonight.

"Now, Lord, please pardon the distraction. See, I've got these two young folks, and they are as welcome as can be, but, Lord, You know my wife. You made her. No need explaining Eloise to You. So what I need to know is this—Sir, what do You want me to do with these two?"

The Good Lord doesn't answer before I get to the crossroads, so I guess it is up to me to decide. I look over at that sleeping girl and see that her left hand is empty. Then, as sure as I'm telling it, I recollect my sister's boy, Tyrell, two towns over in Egypt. Heathen from Hell, if ever I saw one, and I'm talking Bible standards. But I start thinking maybe all that might change once he gets a wife and family. I say wife and family, because it's not just a woman alone that'll straighten him out. Even had a wife for a little while. He's had plenty of women and devilment. But a family, somebody to take to church and maybe do right by, might tempt him to do more good than evil.

Ty is dead to the world when I slip in the door of his little shotgun house. Grass all overgrown and not enough gumption to put up new gutters. That'll change. Nothing like a family to set a man right.

I shake his arm. "Tyrell, Nephew, I brung you a family."

He rubs his bloodshot eyes.

"Son, I'm telling you right now, that this is your chance to get right with God and everybody.   I brung a girl home with me and a . . . " I don't even know what it is. Girl or boy? Baby slept sound the whole way, didn't even dirty its diaper, which seems to me mighty unusual.

" . . . young'un. A ready-made family. All you got to do is meet me over at the Freewill Baptist Chapel in thirty minutes. Take you a bath and be there."

We get over to the Freewill Chapel. Tyrell pulls up right fast behind us.

"What we doing, Preacher?"

"You get in there, Ty," I tell him. "You get on in there and get married."

Nobody is more surprised than me when he does.

Sent Pieces

Georgia StandsStraight Smith Mays Settled

"My brother Ray Allen says we call her Lena," the man who married her tells Georgia. The words slide over her nightgown, a flimsy thing with tiny, nylon bows. "Might as well since she don't already have no name." He leans over Georgia's shoulder to see if she sleeps. "Don't talk much, do you?" Georgia does not answer. Her stiff tongue rests against the roof of her mouth.

"That's fine by me," the man who married Georgia drawls. "Always did like a silent woman."

Silent woman. The words send cold through Georgia's bones. Somewhere along the road to Tennessee, the bus driver passed by a saloon. The sign's painted picture of a naked woman startled Georgia, then sickened her when she realized the woman lacked a head. Silent Woman. That was the name of the tavern.

Georgia starts to shiver, but her body refuses to move.

Christmas comes and the man who married Georgia brings a large pine tree into the front room. He and his brothers track in snow. They toss handfuls of cheap, silver icicles toward the tree. When the icicles hit, they gulp from cans of beer. When they miss, they curse everything they know.

That baby looks like her father.

Since Georgia came to where she is now, she can sit motionless. It is not an affected stillness, but genuine. Her eyes fail to water, and her breathing barely raises her breast. Inertia quells her mind. Nothing happens within its confines. Georgia does not wonder who she was, or why she is here, and as a result, she cannot remember.

Hoarfrost

Oklahoma StandsStraight Waking

I wake up in too much quiet. If you have never been a mother, you will not understand this. You most likely crave silence, pay high rent and pad your home to get it. For mothers, silence is all wrong, a terrible sign of fever, disaster, lack, or lapsed curfew. Too much quiet and you go to looking in bedrooms, peering out windows, hollering names. If you are a mother, I'm not telling you anything you don't know. If you've never been, I could talk all day and never say a thing.

Jack StandsStraight, my husband, is the cause of this quiet. I was a mother once, bore daughters like the best bushes bear roses. Carolina came first.

My husband had only known me a week when he married me. Maybe the revival stirred him up, or maybe it really was the surprise of meeting an girl named Oklahoma in western North Carolina, but Jack walked right up to me and told me that he loved me and that he knew for sure that I was his wife.

Stopped the preacher and told him, too. By sunset the next day, I was a married woman and Jack made me glad about it. We made our daughter Carolina that night and left for Oklahoma the next morning.

There wasn't time to get a doctor. Back then, I couldn't get enough of Jack, followed him everywhere, all the time. Couldn't even sleep good unless he was right there by me. When that first pain came, I was up on one of Jack's horses, trying to like riding as much as he did.

"Jack." I tried to sound as calm as I could. My voice must have betrayed the ache in my body.

"Baby?"

Bloody water gushed down my legs. As it met the ground, a puddle of mud began to form. My husband's eyes widened.

"Jack!" I reached toward him with one hand. He took my hand. Pulling my arm around his neck, Jack slid his other arm under my knees. He picked me up and carried me into the stable.

"Do I need a doctor?"

Jack lifted my skirt. "We ain't got time. We've got us a baby."

My eyes filled with tears. My husband shook his head. "Now, Sugar, there ain't no call for all that. This ain't no different from delivering a colt."

And you know, it wasn't. My husband reached in and took hold. I pushed, once hard, twice harder. He pulled.

My husband was partial to Carolina after that. I apologized to him time after time, on account of not giving him a son, but he just kissed me and said it didn't matter. And it didn't.

My husband carried Carolina with him everywhere. Rigged a flour sack so she could ride on his back. The only time I saw much of her was when he brought her in to eat. After she could eat same as Jack, I hardly ever saw her at all.

That's why Georgia came as such a comfort.   Georgia was all mine. Carolina was her daddy's girl, no doubt in that. She rode horses and played checkers, same as my husband. To tell you the truth, even though I repented, I felt a little left out.

Maybe that's why I wished against a boy. Wrong as it was, I knew that a son would take my husband away from my daughter, and maybe they both would leave me. My husband's dreams would be made of his son, and Carolina and I would be left behind. Way it was, Jack still had to come to me about Carolina, and Carolina would have to come to me for herself. Womanly needs, certain times in her life, would remind her that she had a Mama and had cause to speak with her. If my husband had a son, there'd be no telling.

Georgia was born in my bed. I read the Bible out loud to her, until she was old enough to read it for herself. Her garden grew, her patchwork was perfect and she could cook without a book, the way my Mama did. Maybe that's why I liked her best, in spite of my prayers. Georgia looked like my Mama. Georgia reminded me of home.

Tennessee Jane was a gift. Now, I would never accuse God of showing off, but there are times when I think He likes to remind us of what He can do. Look at peacocks. All those colors and can't even fly. The Smoky Mountains, the Blue Ridge—look at them. Bigger and prettier than whatever man can make and name. Just God reminding us that He's God all by Himself.

That's what I think God did when He made Tennessee Jane. Kind of pretty that makes your breath catch in your throat. And not Hollywood either. Pretty without powder, and pure in heart. Beauty without any danger. That's how I know God had everything to do with making Tennessee Jane.

Here God's good enough to do us a favor, and I forgot to repent of my wishing. All four of my girls were lovely, but Tennessee Jane was spectacular enough to make me forget that I had wished against my husband's son. I bore my last girl before I remembered.

Indiana was the start of quiet. I lost her in a way I can't name, and the house never filled with laughter after that. Jack got bad to drink, and after his truck wreck, well, let's just say, he's been a different man. Carolina stays gone on account of the rodeo, and Tennessee Jane married a traveling preacher. Colton Smith married Georgia, gave me a granddaughter, before he wrecked on black ice and passed away. Georgia took up with trash, wouldn't listen to my pleas to come home. Now, I don't know where my Georgia is, or what became of her daughter.

I want to know. I pray every night and ask God to give me understanding. I ask Him to do whatever He must to let me see my Georgia again. Spare her life. Keep her in her right mind. If she cannot come home on her own, pick her up and bring her back to me.

Jonah's Trouble

Georgia StandsStraight Smith Mays
Wandering

Hell is gastric.
I cannot spell,
And I failed cartography
Two, three times.
One thing I know
North is not South
East and West never meet.
Every compass points toward God
Or Oklahoma.

Against my will
I run standing still
Fill
The belly of the whale
With spiritual indigestion.

Appointed Once

Oklahoma StandStraight Finding

Snow. I look out of the window. It is snowing. Tiny, fine flakes that make the whole world look like one of those cities in a waterglobe. Each snowflake catches the light of the full moon.

I pull the blanket from the bed and wrap it around my shoulders. It's a Pendleton, one that Jack won years ago, in the Herb Jeffries rodeo. I slide my feet into my houseshoes. I mean to watch the snowfall from the window, until I know that I am needed outside.

When I open the door, the cold is the kind that seeps into the bone and stays. I start to shut the door, but for some reason, I look down. What I see startles me.

Georgia. She has fallen, face down, onto the porch. Her hands are stretched toward the door, as if she meant to knock, before she got too cold. Snow has fallen on her back, covered her with a glittering blanket.

My hands dust the snow from my daughter. I cover her with my blanket, which is still warm from my bed.

"Jack!" I call for my husband. "Jack!"

He stumbles out of his bedroom. "What is it?"

"It's Georgia. Help me get her in here, please."

I drag my daughter into the house. Jack rushes to her and picks her up. I shut the door.

"Where you want her? In the front room, by the stove?"

"No, my room." She was born in my bed. If it's her time to die, I want her to be in familiar surroundings. Jack carries her into the small bedroom. As I lift the covers, he places her on the sheet.

"I'll get more blankets," he says.

"I'll get her out of these clothes."

My poor Georgia. Her cotton sweater, her summer dress stood no chance of standing ground against this kind of cold. I peel them away from her. I can see every rib. My flannel nightgown swallows her.

"Georgia? Georgia? This is Mama. Can you hear me?"

No answer.

"That's alright," I tell her. "You can tell me all about it later." Jack brings blankets into the room. We pile them on top of our daughter.

"I put wood on the stove," Jack says. "It should get pretty hot in a minute."

"Thank you," I reply.

"Where you reckon she's been all these years?"

"I don't know, Jack," I answer. "She can tell us about it later."

"See the snow?"

My husband is a man that'll take all your patience. "Yes, Jack. I see it."

"It don't hardly ever snow around here," he tells me. "Reckon she brought it with her?"

"I don't know," I check Georgia's feet and fingers. No frostbite. "Please get me some hot tea. Now's not really the time to think about the weather."

"This ain't weather," Jack continues, "This here is a miracle."

I pick up my hand mirror and place it near Georgia's mouth. She is still breathing.

"A miracle?"

Jack nods. "It's on account of the snow that you got out of the bed. And it's on account of you getting out of bed that you got her in here. It ain't that little bit of snow that made her so cold. She was going cold a long time before."

I start to think Jack may be right. The snow is gone by morning. Jack opens the windows. Georgia shivers.

Flannel. Two gowns. Sixteen blankets. Wool socks. Hot tea.

Georgia sweats ice water.

No matter what we do, we cannot get her warm. My husband stokes the wood stove until both of us are weary from the heat. The doctor comes. He must remove his coat.

"I don't understand," he tells us. "I can barely stand the heat in here. It's warm outside. Yet, she keeps getting colder."

He places a thermometer in her mouth. The mercury moves lazily, until the glass breaks. In a ball, the mercury rolls across the topmost blanket and onto the floor. Jack stops it under his boot.

"Best not to touch that, Jack," warns the doctor. "Do you want to take her to the hospital?"

"No." We turn toward the bed. That's the first word Georgia has said since she returned. Her teeth clatter. "No hospital."

The doctor lifts her wrist. He takes her pulse again.

"How is she, Doc?" My husband's voice sounds hopeful.

The doctor frowns. "Her pulse is far too slow."

"Is it a virus? Is it something we can name?"

"No," the doctor answers me. "She's just too cold."

"No hospital," Georgia says again.

My hand folds over my daughter's. "No hospital. Georgia, listen to me. You're cold. We need to get you warm. Do you have any idea what is wrong with you?"

"Mama?"

"Yes, Georgia?"

"What happened to Nathan Hollow?" My husband and the doctor exchange troubled glances.

"Nathan Hollow? Why would he matter to you?"

"Mama, I need to know what happened to him."

"Well—"

"Cut his own throat with a razor," my husband blurts out. "Bled out in the back of his ice truck."

Georgia's teeth stop clattering. "Oh," she says, as if we just told her the whole duty of man or something. "Oh."

All of a sudden, my daughter's hand is warm around mine. I put my other hand on her forehead. The beginning of warm answers my palm.

"Mama," Georgia says, "will you please take away these blankets? It's mighty hot in here."

My husband and I lift the blankets from her body. We take them into the hallway, so that the doctor can examine my daughter.

"Why did you tell her that about Nathan Hollow?" I ask Jack.

Jack shrugs. "If she was that near to dying and that's how she used her last breath, it must have been something she needed to know."

"I can't imagine anybody needing to know something awful as that."

"Well," says Jack, "at least it got her warm."

Three hours later, I am sitting with Georgia. She is finally warm enough. I have given her a bath, made sure she knew how much I love her.

"Georgia," I ask. "What happened to the baby?"

"What baby?"

I take her hand in mine. "Your baby, Precious."

"Oh." Georgia's eyes are blank. "She's dead."

My eyes water. I kiss my daughter's hand again and again. "Georgia, Precious, I'm so very sorry. Where did you bury her?"

Georgia smiles, a wan smile, at me. "In Egypt."

I figure my daughter is talking out of her head. I climb into the bed and put my arms around her thin frame. I fall asleep first. I wake again in a little while, but Georgia never does.

Shopping in Egypt

Lena Allen Mays Talking

You want to talk about me, you got to talk about Cumberland. Cumberland is a boxer dog, and about the best way I can make you see him is to tell you he looks exactly like a marshmallow right off the campfire. You know what I mean. Let's say you have a marshmallow, the super-duper, jumbo kind and you toast it. Well, if you handle your stick right, it'll get a little bit brown all around and then dark charcoal at the front.

That's how Cumberland is.

Jimmy and Ray Allen, my father's half-brothers, are sheriffs of adjoining counties, this one and the next one over. On the other side, Daddy's first wife's brother, Donald, is deputy sheriff, so Daddy makes sure not to drive drunk over there. Jimmy and Ray Allen understand. Ol' Donald, he's waiting on an opportunity.

Anyhow, the Governor of Kentucky was up late one night, and he saw how these prisons in Florida were training up dogs to sniff out cocaine and explosives and stuff like that. The most interesting part was how the federal government was handing out grant money to any county that wanted to get some dogs and teach them how to bark when they smelled illegal drugs. Next thing we knew, Jimmy and Ray Allen were coming back with a carload of dogs they got from Shoot, my aunt Rayetta's brother. Rayetta is Ray Allen's wife.

And no, we ain't inbred, it's just a coincidence that Ray Allen and his wife's got names so close. Actually, that's how Ray Allen knew he was supposed to marry her. He likes to tell that story every Thanksgiving, right before him and Daddy get all the way drunk, how he walked into Johnson's General Store to get undershirts and walked out with red-haired, freckled Rayetta. Her daddy about took a fit, until Ray Allen got himself elected sheriff. I say got himself elected because, around here, democracy is relative, and Ray Allen happened to have more relatives registered to vote than ol' Alphabet Jackson. They called him Alphabet because, instead of reading folks their rights, he'd go to reciting the alphabet. That's on account of him not knowing how to read. But that's neither sticks nor stones since he choked on a neckbone last Decoration Day.

So Ray Allen and Jimmy got all these dogs and time-and-a-half pay. Most of the dogs seemed alright enough for all practical purposes, lying out in the sun and growling at convicts. But Cumberland was a different story. He was smart enough alright, he just had other ideas. Cumberland had ambition.

While the other dogs shivered out in the cold, Cumberland would walk right up to the deputy on duty and lie down on his feet. Who could throw that outside?

The other dogs? Feed them scraps and possum and they'd be ready for a nap. Cumberland? He'd end up eating off your plate. Even if you were behind bars. Cumberland visited the jail cell regularly, partly so he could get his head petted, and the other part so he could get the rest of the biscuits and gravy off the miscreant's plate.

Fact is, I never did know how they got to calling him Cumberland. Might have come with him from where he came from, or maybe somebody just started it and didn't quit. Anyway, all you had to do was say his name and he'd be right there. Just like that. Ray Allen got real partial to him.

One night, Ray Allen come by and picked up Daddy. It wasn't until they were all the way gone that I noticed sugar on the floor. Now Daddy ain't Fannie Farmer, and he drinks his coffee black, and spilled sugar could only signify one thing. See, I keep the house money away from Daddy in the strangest places, on account of when he drinks, he spends it all up. I fold twenties into triangles and slide them between my bed and box spring. Tens go in the sugar, salt, deep in the flour. Anything bigger, I sew into pillows, stuff into wherever I can remember Daddy hasn't been. This time, I got in a hurry and put it all in the sugar. Which, as I mentioned, is now on the floor.

Cussing won't bring back currency, which is what Mama used to say. I don't recall my Mama too much, except that she used to sit entirely still. I mean, still. I know people say set still or keep still, but even then, they aren't altogether still. Now, Mama, she was still. All that let you know she was alive was her breathing. Even that—her chest moved just enough to exchange air without disrupting anything else. Daddy said that's how come he didn't notice when she was gone, she was all the time so still. Me personally, I think it's more likely he didn't notice because he was all the time so drunk.

So when I see the sugar, I know what Daddy's done. I'm fit to be tied by the time he and Ray Allen pull up in front of our shotgun house. Shotgun, they call it, on account of if you shot a gun at the front door, the bullet would come out at the back. Well, I'm certain that if I shoot Daddy's rifle at the front stoop, the bullet will surely hit Ray Allen's Ford pickup. I pick up the gun and walk outside. I step through the frame of what used to be a screened door.

"Hey, Baby." Daddy slurs this.

"Where is the house money?" I am not fooling.

Daddy looks at the gun. He smiles at me. I do not smile at him. My eyes narrow.

"Baby," he begins, "you are not going to believe this . . . "

"No, I'm not," I told him. "You might as well save your breath and your soul."

I can see Daddy thinking, deciding for or against a lie.

"Well, Lena," mumbles Ray Allen, who named me after Lena Horne, who he swore up and down was a real angel from Heaven. That is until he found out she was Colored. He about had a fit then, but it was too late, I was named. It never bothered me none, Colored or not, I never saw anything as beautiful. Well, I did, once. Once we drove past the Colored part of town and there was a girl, I think, not quite a woman, walking along the side of the road. She had the thickest, blackest hair I'd ever seen, next to skin the color of raw honey. But that wasn't what made her so beautiful.

When Daddy and Jimmy honked the horn at her to get out of the road, she looked up. She had these eyes, these eyes I can't forget. I don't even recall the color, they were so striking. They were clean. Clean. I mean, everybody's life is written in their eyes. You ever seen somebody who carried everything they ever done with them?

Then you hear that they're only twenty or something, but can't believe it since they look twice that old. That's a hard kind of twenty and it's all in the eyes.

Well, this girl, there was nothing in her eyes. Nothing. No shame. No regret. No dread. No nothing. Just clean.

After we passed her by, I asked Jimmy what her name was. Sao, he told me. Her folks were Portuguese, Spanish, something like that. Colored, but not quite. Too colored to be white trash, like folks call us, but not colored enough to be Colored for real.

Thing was, he said it almost respectful. Said Sao had some strange ways, but that she had a lot of power. Like once, when it didn't rain for ages, she went over to the capitol with some preachers and prayed for rain. All of them hollered a while, but the sky didn't bust wide open until Sao walked right up and said, "Please." Just "please." Jimmy said it rained for weeks after that. Folks thought they might have to get Sao back over to the capitol to make it quit.

"Ty, let me handle this," Ray Allen clears his throat. "Lena, I know you're upset."

"I am so much more than upset, Ray Allen."

Daddy grins at me. "Well, at least you're not giving us the silent treatment." I don't even let him finish. I can hear the rest—like your Mama used to. He has himself some nerve.

"No, I'm not. I am giving you the shooting treatment."

I lift the rifle. I mean it this time. Steal the house money, and then talk about Mama? That is just uncalled-for.

"We bought you a present," Daddy is clearly stalling for time.

"And what is that?" I am choosing which one to shoot at first. One thing about me, I am a very sure shot. That is why I am only going to wing them, rather than wound them. They both need to go back to work next Monday so we can pay the light bill.

Daddy looks at Ray Allen. Ray Allen looks back, like Simple Simon or something. They don't either have any kind of present for me. This level of sorriness cannot be tolerated. I need to shoot both of them and the tires on general principle.

Ray Allen looks like he just got a bright idea. I halfway expect a cartoon lightbulb to appear over his head.

"Lena, look," he says. He opens the back of door of the truck and lifts out something. When he puts it on the ground, I can see that whatever it is, it's alive. A dog. It shakes its head and walks right over to me.

"His name's Cumberland," Ray Allen tells me.

"That's a fact," Daddy chimes in, as if he knew.

"He's a boxer," Ray Allen adds.

"Looks like a dog to me," I answer. I am not altogether over the idea of shooting them or the truck.

"That's a kind of dog," Ray Allen replies.

"Sure enough," says Daddy.

I look down at the dog, and as much as I miss the house money, I like ol' Cumberland in spite of myself.

"Hello, Cumberland," I greet him, "I hope you're worth ninety-two dollars."

Cumberland sits down and smiles at me. Really. From ear to ear.

I decide against shooting my kinfolks. At least for the time being.

From then on, Cumberland and I have been insepara-ble. I still went to school then, until I missed so many days that I had Daddy sign for me to drop out as soon as I turned sixteen. That makes three years Cumberland and I have been together and alone with Daddy.

I say that on account of living with Daddy is like living with nobody and a whole bunch of people all at the same time. Like living in a monkey puzzle, Mama would say. You go in one way and everything hits you from seven ways. The lights don't get cut off, but the well needs a new pump. The pump gets bought, and then Daddy gets laid off. Everybody gets laid off, except Ray Allen, who keeps getting elected. That's on account of his forgiving attitude toward his electorate driving while less than sober. There's only really one place to work in this town, the Greenly Plant, and it moved its operations to Mexico.

Daddy's unemployment check comes in regular, and I go with him to cash it. Then I give him twenty dollars back and hide the rest. Too much free time and he's liable to spend it all in one place. Me, I do what I always done. Make a dollar out of fifteen cents, put supper on the table and watch TV. We only get one station on account of we can't afford cable, but it has most of the talk shows on in the afternoon. I sit there with Cumberland and look at how stupid the people are. There they are in Chicago, New York, Los Angeles. They could get a job right after the taping and never even look back at their sorry lives. That's what I'd do. I just wonder if the hosts would let me bring Cumberland.

Most nights, Cumberland sleeps with me. I don't have a bed frame, just the box spring and mattress on the floor. That's good, since Cumberland's legs are short. He gets up on the foot of the bed, on my side, and lays there a while. About the time I finish brushing my teeth, he scoots over to the other side. That way, my feet have a warmed spot when I get in. I truly appreciate that kind of thoughtfulness.

Cumberland and Daddy never have too much to say to each other. I feed Cumberland first thing in the morning, and Daddy doesn't get out of bed 'til around noon.

Cumberland always sniffs at the air when Daddy comes into the front room, on account of the alcohol coming off Daddy's pores. Daddy drinks black coffee, takes a shower, and goes out for the rest of the day. I don't ask where. As long as the house money's safe, I'm not so sure I much care.

Cumberland and I do this and that. One thing about Cumberland, he sure is neat. Never had a flea. Not a mange spot on him. When he goes outside to do his business, he wipes his feet on the way in. He does. He stands right on this rubber mat marked *Welcome* that I got for Daddy's boots when he worked over at Greenly. Cumberland has never tracked in mud, even when I have.

Most days, I straighten up the house. Then, I watch my shows. Lately, I have taken to writing down words that sound important, words that a quality person would say. I write them in a spiral book left from my basic math class. Dysfunctional, contradictory, eradicate—all these I learned from my shows. I repeat them to Cumberland until I get the sound of them right.

Marthal, Jimmy's wife, comes by once in a while. She never comes in, just leaves magazines from her church and copies of the *Holiness Quarterly*. Holiness people don't believe in television. A "one-eyed devil," the *Holiness Quarterly* calls it. I offer to turn it off, but Marthal says she can't stay. Something about light and darkness getting along.

Funny thing about it, Marthal looks like a movie star. Not like the come-and-go people out now, but like a real movie star, back when it meant something, like at MGM. Her skin is like milk, not a spot on her, and she has auburn hair that she piles on top of her head. Her dresses reach clear down to the floor, like she fell off a covered wagon. Jimmy's so proud of her having religion and all,

says he can trust her when he's off guarding the county. I
think he's just glad he has a woman he can run around on
without her leaving him or talking back. If I looked like
Marthal, me and Cumberland would move to Hollywood.

Daddy comes in late Thursday night and gets up early.
The day is gray and rainy, so I hope that won't keep him
home. My shows look good today. One is the rest of a
two-parter, where girls finally find out who daddied their
babies. Another is all about lifestyles of very rich people.
The other is about people who won the lottery and lost it
all. As far as I can see, people like that just qualified themselves for lifetime pensions as their local idiot.

"Lena," Daddy starts off shaky. Usually, he doesn't
even talk until after he's had his coffee.

"Yeah?"

"Lena, I was wondering if you could let me have a little of the house money . . . "

Of course. That's it. "Sorry, Daddy. There's nothing left
until you get your next check." I am not really lying.
Everything left is owed out, which means it really belongs
to someone else.

"Nothing? Not even a little bit?"

"Unh-uh. In fact, I was wondering if you could have
Ray Allen run me over to Johnson's to pay the light bill."

Sudden, sharp pain wraps around the side of my head.
Daddy has hit me. Hard.

"So you do have money," he hollers. "I won't have you
lying to me, girl!"

My eyes hurt. I can't believe I let it slip about the house
money.

"Where is it?" Daddy hits me again. He calls me all out
of my name. From behind him, I hear Cumberland growl.

"I won't be disrespected in my own house!"

Daddy pulls me by the arm. He opens the door and drags me out through it. Cumberland bites him on the leg. Daddy cusses us both as he pushes me forward. The gravel of the driveway scratches my palms as I try to brace myself. Daddy is kicking, trying to get loose of Cumberland. Blood seeps through Daddy's pantsleg. Finally, Daddy kicks Cumberland for real. He jumps into Ray Allen's truck and backs away.

What I see next makes me scream.

Daddy has ran over Cumberland. Tire tracks and grease and rain and blood tie-dye the grass and gravel. I rush up to Cumberland and about slip in yet another mess Daddy has made.

"Oh, Cumberland," I tell him. This is the thing I was saying before, just how Cumberland has the best dog disposition ever. His side is split open, the skin pulled back like you'd scale walleye or trout, and what I can see is raw and red. Still, he wags his tail, slow, when I get down on my knees beside him. In all that red, I see white and I know that Daddy has hurt us to the bone.

"Oh Cumberland," I say again. About all I can do is moan. Cumberland licks the side of my hand, between the thumb and forefinger, and I about go to bawling right there. I slide my sweatshirt over my head and lay it across Cumberland. Before I do, I pick up Cumberland's skin and pull it over the rest of him.

"Cumberland, I'm going for Sao." I say this like he'll understand, which I think he will. One thing about Cumberland, he's always been a way above average kind of smart. Compared to other dogs, he's some kind of regional genius. That's why I think he's never been much to mingle with the local dogs, who just run here and there and mate and get mated. Cumberland was always above that.

I run, keep running toward the Bottoms. It's over past the railroad tracks, where most of the Coloreds and Mexicans live. I don't even know Sao's last name, and Daddy says don't never cross them tracks or I'll skin you alive, but I figure he just skinned Cumberland, and anybody who can tell it to rain and it does can probably get God to rescue my dog.

When I get across the tracks, there is the cleanest, sweetest house you'd ever want to see. It looks exactly like a peppermint, whitewashed white and lined out in red. Red. I think about Cumberland, and I think this must be it, this must be the right house.

As it turns out, Sao has been thinking before me. She is out standing in front of the front steps. There is a plaster rooster by the porch and some of those plants they call hens and chicks. When I used to dream about a real home for me and Cumberland, this is what I meant, and Sao lives in it. And there she is, standing in the rain, in the prettiest green slicker you'd ever want to see. Like some kind of mountain princess, just waiting. Waiting for me.

"Who is it?" she asks, just like that, just like she seen me on my way coming.

"Cumberland," I tell her, "will you come?"

She doesn't answer, even though she don't know Cumberland from Christmas, just starts running right behind me, keeping up like she knows the way. We get to the house and there's Cumberland, breathing hard like he's been running. Or ran over. Sao gets right down on the ground by him and I can see her skirt. Pale pink, like it's gone to blushing, but it's soaking up blood and motor grease now. I start to say something, but she's already talking to Cumberland.

"Cumberland," she says softly, and his eyes open. For a moment I am almost jealous, but I need whatever she does to save Cumberland.

"Do you want me to take off the sweatshirt?" I ask her. She doesn't even know how bad it is. She shakes her head, and the hood of her raincoat throws off water. Her lips are moving. One word—"Please."

Cumberland barks. Sao stands up just like that and I throw myself down on the ground. Cumberland licks my face. I reach over and peel back the sweatshirt. Cumberland's skin is back on. Not even a seam. His tail is wagging.

"Oh Cumberland!" I hug my dog as tight as I know how. His little body squirms, not to get away, but to show how happy he is. I laugh and I cry and Cumberland licks my face. I am not teasing when I tell you his breath smells like roses.

I don't think to thank Sao for a good while. When I do, she's gone.

The first thing I do, I look for the house money. All that ruckus and Daddy had already found it in the back of the *Holiness Quarterly* anyway. That means the lights get cut off. Serves Daddy right. Next, I put me some iodine on my scratches. Dirt has ground itself into the wound. That's the way the worst hurts are, all kinds of filth down under the scars.

All afternoon, I pack Cumberland's dog dishes and my clothes in plastic bags. There isn't any money. We can't stay here with Daddy, but I don't know where we should go. I look at the front cover of the *Holiness Quarterly* that I thought was keeping the house money safe. "There is a Promised Land," it says.

"Yes," I ask nobody in particular, "but is there a map?"

It's right then that Daddy comes in, like nothing's gone wrong, like he didn't take all the house money and Cumberland ain't been ran over. He smiles, and I notice he's going long in the tooth. That's how drinking does, sugars over the teeth before it eats up the mind and the liver.

"How's my baby?" Daddy hands me a box marked *Sweeties*. It weighs a good three pounds if it weighs anything. "Them's the best chocolates there is," he says, making a declaration like candy will make up for us getting robbed by family and Cumberland getting ran over. Dogs can't even eat chocolate.

Cumberland stands up. I pick up my plastic bags from by the door.

"Daddy, me and Cumberland are through with you."

I say it just like that. Not a peep out of Daddy, because he knows we mean it. I walk out the door. Cumberland follows me. We keep walking, heel-toe, heel-toe, paw-after-paw, until we forget here.

What You Wish For

Love Felíz Skenadore Allied

Staralee hit an owl on the way over. Bad enough to hit an owl, but this one was a baby.

"You know I hit an owl," she tells me, as I get in the passenger's side of her Ford Escort. Staralee's real proud of this car—first thing she bought when our tribe got the casino and sliced the cash pie into hundreds of pieces. That's how I see it, too, casino checks are like slivers of pie from Calliotte's Family Diner, wrapped in paper napkins and mailed general delivery, cherries and coconut cream spilling out of the envelope and into the hands of car dealers and guys that sell beer and trailers.

Anyhoo, Staralee keeps the white car spotless. The outside, that is. The inside is a pit. Pop bottles and enough dust to choke the vacuum. Yet, Staralee runs it through the car wash every time she gets enough gas to go past the front yard. I can just imagine the blue streak she cussed trying to get owl blood off the hood.

"Whole lot of blood for a junior-sized owl," she growls. Only instead of saying "whole lot," she swears. "Sorry, Love."

People always look at us sideways when they hear her say that, like they think we might be funny or something.

Years ago, I'd take the time to explain that's my legal name. Love. Love Felíz Skenadore. Now, I just glare at them. I've never seen any of them pay the bills at my mom and dad's house.

Staralee says one of those things that makes it impossible to get mad at her. "I wish I would think before I open my mouth. I keep forgetting you go to church."

"Where you should be," I answer. "You know, you don't need no ticket. They let everybody in the door." This is an old conversation. We have it every time she swears. And the results always come back the same. Staralee doesn't darken the door of Saint Dominic's.

Still, she brings me ten percent of everything she makes, and I put it in the collection box. Somebody taught her to do that, and so far she's never wrecked a car or had trouble with her blood sugar. She looks like she's paying the premiums on a heavenly insurance plan.

"I would, but I was reading the *National Inquiry* this week . . . "

If there's one thing Staralee knows, it's what the *National Inquiry* had to say this week. That and what happened on *Hope for Tomorrow*.

"I don't know, Love," she goes on. "Going to church might be getting pretty dangerous. *National Inquiry* had an article about some wacko that's been writing threatening letters to churches. He's calling himself the First Horseman or something."

"Where is this exactly?" Life has taught me there's two kinds of people. Interpreters and recorders. Interpreters hear what you say, but care more about what you mean than about quoting you word-for-word. Ask a recorder what just went on, and you get a recitation. I think Staralee's an interpreter, but she's usually pretty accurate with her details, even when she's got the main idea wrong.

"Oh, West Virginia, Mississippi, someplace," Staralee gestures with her right hand. Staralee always did drive left-handed.

"Alabama? We're in Green Bay!"

Staralee nods. Her thick, black braid swings. "Yeah, but you know how things like that trickle up."

"Down, Staralee, down. Like from New York City. Like from Chicago. Never has anybody heard of anything trickling up from Beckley or Biloxi. I mean, when have you ever in your life heard anybody say, 'that's the way they do it in Beckley, West Viriginia, and we absolutely got to do it that way here, too?"

Staralee shrugs. "You never know."

I'm pretty sure we do. At least about this, we do. I take Staralee's cue and change the subject.

"You think we should still go? I mean, with the owl and all?" Mama used to tell me, don't borrow trouble. Still says that. Said it the other day, when I first told her we were going to get a good look at this girl who's messing with Staralee's husband. I mean, I can't let her go through this thing all by herself.

After all, Staralee and I have been together since the first day at Miss Barksdale's Head Start. She was a Star then, and I'm a Skenadore, so we sat by or close to each other every school day of our lives. Her family was fresh off the Oneida reservation, and my daddy had been off it ever since he met Mom at church in Green Bay. The Spanish Mass was at 8:00 A.M. All the Indians went at 9:15. Dad got it backwards and sat through the whole early service, thinking that it must be for some other tribe or something. I think he sat through it mainly for Mom, who sang in the choir. She sang *Ave Maria* all by herself that day. Dad said it was like swallowing a pill for his loneliness. He married her three months later.

"Things God does don't take much time," he says. I don't have the heart to bring up the forty years in the wilderness or the Bablyonian captivity. Besides, Staralee and Damon got married two weeks after graduation, and up to this mess, they've been alright. I've got to hand it to Dad, he and Mom are as happy as they can be.

"Don't borrow trouble," Mom warns. But next time we go to Mass, she lights a candle to Saint Anne, next to the usual ones for Saint Dismas and the Sacred Heart of Jesus. She sees me looking at the candle and pats my cheek.

"A baby would settle Staralee down. Damon, too."

A baby. I can't bring myself to tell Mom that's what we're talking about. Staralee looked over the hang-up calls and Damon's late nights and saw that Damon was running around.

Strangest thing, too, since he was good as gold to Staralee all during high school. Treated her like a queen. You know, the kind of guy that got his bow tie and cumberbund to match her prom dress. The type that always wanted to stop at those machines where you go in and get a comic strip of instant pictures. Put them up in his locker. Got tags airbrushed for his van—"Staralee and Damon 4-EVER." Wears her class ring around his neck to this day.

Staralee don't even have to work, which Mom says is half her problem. She doesn't have anything much to do all day except read *National Inquiry* and listen to Damon's mom.

"That's where all this trouble started," Mom tells me. "Staralee's got a good man and a good life and people can't stand that. Got to meddle and instigate. What Staralee needs to do is look at those paychecks Damon brings home like clockwork and get to working on a baby."

Don't even worry about that girl, I told Staralee. I said it over and over. But during her perm the other day, the girl under the other dryer told Staralee that that girl's been telling everybody who'll listen that she's got Damon's baby. That's what hurt Staralee. She and Damon been married two whole years now, and no baby. Staralee doesn't say much about it, but she cuts out every article about infants and being pregnant that the *National Inquiry* prints.

One time, we drove over to Wal-Mart and wandered up and down the aisles. I went to use the bathroom, and when I came out, there was Staralee with her arms around a baby doll. Every time she squeezed it, it cried, "Mama." Staralee's back was to me. She hugged that doll one last time, and sat it on the shelf. When she wiped her eyes on her coat sleeve, I went back in the restroom and cried.

"What's wrong? You superstitious?" Staralee asks. Then she does one of the other things that makes it impossible to stay aggravated at her. She turns on the heat, high as it'll go, and makes sure all the blowers are facing towards me. I am always too cold. Staralee worries that it might be my circulation.

"I thought you were." A lot of Indians think owls are bad luck. A death in the family. And Staralee's family is way into that old-time Indian stuff. Real blanket Indians, my dad would say.

"Well," she shrugs, "I figure I hit an owl. A *baby* owl. That's got to be some kind of sign or something."

"Maybe a sign we should not go."

"Too late." We pull up at the gas station. It has a Polish—German kind of name from a country where all the people are all the way white.

"We don't have to go in."

"You don't. I do." Staralee opens her door and slams it behind her. She comes around to my side and pulls the door handle. "Listen, Love, you wait out here. I just want to see."

Seeing doesn't take but a minute. Staralee gets back in the car, shuts the door, and turns the key in the ignition.

"She says it's his."

My hand clasps Staralee's right arm. "You don't know that, Hon. You don't. I mean, all you know is it's another white girl—some trash from Kentucky come up here to work at the casino—claiming she's going to have a brown baby that'll get a dividend check every year. This is Green Bay. Oneida is three miles from the border. This means less than nothing."

"I know it's his."

"You don't know any such thing. At least, not for sure."

"*He* says it's his."

My mouth waters, sour, like before you get sick. Warm and bitter take turns at the back of my tongue.

"Damon? Damon, your husband, Damon, says it's his?"

Staralee's right hand reaches for the glove compartment. I open it and hand her two napkins from Gerri's Dairy Twist. She blows her nose, crumples the napkins, and tosses them on the floor.

"Is my nose messy?" She turns her head as much as she can and still keep her eyes on the road.

"You look fine. You *knew* it was Damon's?"

"He told me. Said he wants to give it his name, since we don't have kids of our own. Don't look like we ever will."

My father's mother lost her eyes to diabetes. Her hearing left her years before. Yet her fingers could still weave baskets. I feel something weaving my stomach into knots, a basket of bile under my goosedown jacket.

"People go through stuff like this and get through it. You should come talk to Father Demain at church. You guys get some counseling, and I bet you have your own baby in a year."

Staralee shakes her head. She sighs. "Remember that party graduation night? The one you weren't allowed to go to?"

"You weren't either."

"Well, I went anyway. Went with Damon. He got pretty wasted. I never had seen him like that before. He thought I was flirting with Charley Reece. He pretty much beat him down. Then, he . . . well . . . he came after me. I was messed up for a week."

"I thought you went to your granny's!"

"I did. After I went to the hospital. A couple days later, I got out. The doctor told my mom and dad that my insides were all bruised up, and well . . . it didn't look good. My dad and my two brothers went over and had a, well, a *talk* with Damon. We got married a couple weeks later."

"*That*, I knew. *This*, I didn't." It is something shocking how you can know somebody like the back of your hand one minute and the next minute find out you don't know them at all.

"Don't be mad, Love. It didn't matter. I thought it didn't. Well, maybe it did."

We ride back across town in silence. Staralee pulls up in front of my mom and dad's house. She leaves the car running. Most days, she comes on in and stays a while. Damon's mom usually cooks dinner.

"You coming in?" I ask her.

She shakes her head no. "Reach in my purse," she orders.

I do. My fingers find a tiny, tiny basket. I pull it out and look at it.

"What is this?"

"That, Love, is the answer to my marital problems."

The knots in my stomach pull tighter. "What do you mean, Staralee?"

"I went to see that Ease woman."

"Molly Ease? She's a witch!"

"Maybe."

"I thought you didn't believe in all that stuff."

"I don't. But she came highly recommended."

"By who? Hell?"

Staralee rolls her eyes at me. Tears have melted her eyeliner into her mascara. I reach over and wipe under her eye with my thumb.

"Staralee, do you even know what this stuff is? What it does? I mean, I'd leave that Indian magic alone if I was you."

"I don't need to know what it is. Molly promised it will only help, not hurt. All I need to do is put this basket under Damon's pillow tonight. From that moment on, she says he will see nothing but me."

"I don't know, Staralee. We could get my mom to pray about it first. We could even go to church our ownselves and pray. Maybe ask Father Demain what he thinks we ought to do."

"What good will that do?"

"Okay, Staralee, maybe that doesn't seem like much right now. We've had a weird day. Maybe a weird life, even. But you hit an owl. Now, you've got this basket. Just promise me you won't do anything until we talk about it some more."

Staralee agrees. "You know, even though he's treated me like . . . well, you know what I mean, did me dirty like this, I still love him. He's all I've got. Maybe all I'll ever have. He can't leave me."

I'm too busy trying not to vomit to answer. Staralee leans over me and opens the door. I put my arms around her and hug her, as tight as I can. When I get out of the car, she throws it into reverse. The tires squeal as she leaves the driveway.

Mom asks me how my day was. I tell her it was fine. She goes back to stirring chili to go with tonight's fry-bread. Indian tacos. Mom still eats the Mexican kind. I can't eat anything at dinner. I go to bed early. Mom offers to leave some pop out, so I can drink it once it loses the fizz. Dad leaves and comes back with lime sherbet, the kind I used to like when I was little. Mom says if this keeps up, we're going by the hospital tomorrow. We can bypass the general clinic if Dad's sister is working. She makes the appointments.

I tell them that I am not really sick, which I am not, but I do not tell them that I am sad. That would worry them way more than if I was sick. Mom would probably rush right over to church, and there is no saint that can right all this wrong.

Mom shakes my shoulder at four in the morning. Staralee's mother called. There is terrible trouble. They are going to the hospital. Dad is going to drive us all over there. He drives so fast that the whole world seems to be moving very slowly.

Dad drops us off at the door and goes to find a parking space. Mom heads straight to the hospital chapel. I go to the ER. Damon is flat on his back, on a gurney, moaning. White bandages wrap his head. Blood seeps from what used to be his eyes.

Staralee rises from the hard plastic chair. Her eyes are rimmed with red from crying. She holds onto me for a moment.

"What happened, Staralee?"

"I'm not sure," she answers, using a voice that's a little too loud, like people do around foreigners and people who can't see. She opens her brown hand. When I see that little basket, I know all I need to know.

Fail for Watching

Lena Allen Mays Scheming

I am sitting in the room I rent over Phillippi's gas station when somebody knocks. When I open the door, there is a Colored girl in front of me. Mexican, Indian, some type of girl I wouldn't even speak to back in Kentucky.

"I've come about the baby," she says.

Ain't no baby. I read how every one of these Indians gets a check off the casino profits every year. I figured Damon would be easy pickings, and he was. Especially once he told me that he wanted a baby more than anything. Before he got his eyes put out, a baby or two by him would've been better than welfare.

"You Damon's wife?"

"No. I'm his wife's best friend. And the way I figure it, you're in my best friend's way."

Not no more, I think. I'm not hardly going to fight anybody over some cripple.

"And what are you offering me to move?"

The girl looks startled, like she was expecting more of a fight. She motions toward the tiny window.

"Look down there. You get in that car down there. Drive off, and don't ever come back."

Sold. Me and Cumberland would have gone back to Kentucky a long time ago, if we'd had a way to get there.

The girl holds out the title, signed already, and hands the keys to me. I take Cumberland and my jacket and walk down the stairs. I get into the car and drive away. I see the state line of Kentucky before I remember that I never told anybody there goodbye.

The Marriage of Saints

Sao Espiritu Confirming

If I am a saint, I was born one. The third daughter of a third daughter, I broke the continuity of girls named Sao in just one way. I was wanted.

My parents, Juan Henry Espiritu and Sao Fuego Espiritu, like every other set of parents in our part of Kentucky, had good sense enough to know they wanted a boy. Boys are easier to raise everybody says, and it certainly costs less. For our family, living on commodity cans of potted meat and what could be peaches or pears, boys made better sense than girls. Instead of spending the seasonal income that my daddy made drilling wells on ruffled dresses and patent leather Mary Janes, they could buy socks and T-shirts and hope for the best. Boys could be turned out into the future to make their way, but girls required watching until they were safely folded into taffeta and lace and given away in plain view of the Messiah, all the saints, and every great-aunt that could count backwards from nine.

So it was a son they were wanting when Mamí bent double over her sewing machine. Clutching her belly, clawing at nothing, she delivered a daughter, eight months along and perfect. Only one thing marred the beauty of her delicate eyelashes and her tiny fingernails, complete with opal half-moons at their base. She never breathed. Mamí and Papí called her Sao and buried her in the family plot over at Our Hope of Perpetual Help Church. The whole thing hurt, but they were young and there was plenty of time, or so everyone said.

Eighteen months later, my mother went into labor. They were weeding the garden, trying to grow potatoes. My mother struck the earth with a hoe three times and bent over. Sao Number Two slid into the world 186 seconds after the hoe fell to the ground. According to my father, who told it to his mother Rhoda, Sao the Second breathed exactly twice and sighed. "She never did open her eyes," Papí told Abuelita.

"Too good for this world," was always how Abuelita finished the story.

It was just about all my parents could take. On his way home from burying my second sister, Papí stopped in the vestibule of the Our Lady of Perpetual Help Church and stood amidst the gallery of wax saints that stared beatifically into a glory that none of us could see.

Papí balled up his fists and cried out,"If any of you are listening, tell God to give me a child!" Well, I was born in County General exactly nine months later. Papí never could tell which of the saints it was that was listening, or even if it was God Himself, but he always gave credit to Saint Dominic, on account of he was standing right in front of his statue when he hollered out like that.

Back to the saint situation, being the third girl of a third girl gave it sort of a mystical quality. Add to all that being born on All Saints' Day just about convinced Mamí and Abuelita that all the saints had helped in my conception, which meant that I must be as much saint as sinner, to say the least.

Saintliness and madness appear to be close cousins. About three weeks into the third grade, the class pet—a hamster named Sid—died after Rob Adams dropped him on the ground. The other girls screamed and the boys looked out for blood, but I scooped Sid up in my palm.

"Oh God," I asked, "please make Sid live again."

Remarkably, the rodent started breathing, his little hamster lungs puffing out small sighs. The other children clapped. I was just as surprised as anybody in the room. My teachers sent a note home. I played well with others, they said, but my religious zeal raised red flags of caution. By the time of my thirteenth birthday, I was well known in Egypt, Kentucky, and all the way over in Cast Salt for dreaming things that came to pass. Miss Kennewick, the high school counselor, suggested to Mamí that I might have been a little left-of-stable.

Mamí disagreed, called it persecution on account of my saintly tendencies. She carried me over to the Independent Baptist Church, but they warned her that all this trouble comes from worshiping idols and praying to Jesus' mother. Mamí repented and drove around in circles, until she found herself way out in Perryville, right in front of a big tent. Like a circus tent, only nothing is funny that goes on underneath. A lean, spare man in a night-colored suit stood in the front, shouting about the close proximity of hellfire. Hundreds of people moaned, lifting their hands and shouting right along with him.

For Mamí, sainthood is a simple thing. It is a condition, like being born with flat feet or favoring your left hand. Attending Flaming Fire Pentecostal Christian Church on the Rock does not endanger my saintly status in the least. In fact, when I become a missionary, it only helps.

Saul of Tarsus fell off his horse and Saint Matthew walked off his job. God calls me while I fold laundry.

Sleeve to sleeve, once over, I fold Papí's cotton T-shirts. He is not particular about much except laundry. White means white, he says. Mamí figures that my nearness to sainthood means that my robe in Heaven will be the whitest of all of ours, so she delegates the washing to me. I am on my third shirt when I hear, big as day, "Indians." Well, I hear it in the kind of voice that makes you not even care if the laundry wrinkles. I fall on the ground and begin to weep, great big tears that would make a crocodile jealous. Only I mean every one.

"Oh God," I sob, wiping my eyes on one of Papí's prized T-shirts, "I don't want to go to India. I don't want to go so far away from Mamí and Papí and Abuelita and Mammaw. But I will, Lord Jesus, I'll go anywhere you want me to go."

It is right then that God talks to me. Right out loud. Like the sound of water all running together at the same time. "Who said anything about India? I said Indians." Now you can believe that if you want to, it doesn't change my life if you don't. This is my story, and I'm telling you how it happened.

Mamí and Papí are so proud they are about to bust. They clap their hands together, shouting that now I am a shoo-in for Heaven. They hug each other and run around talking about how their girl is worth three boys. Mamí, who is part Creek Indian herself, is just about beside herself with joy.

"Let's go on over to the church and celebrate," Papí says. They grab jackets and go out the door, headed over to the third night of revival at the Flaming Fire Pentecostal Christian Church on the Rock. Papí suggests that they stop by Our Hope of Perpetual Help Church and thank all the saints on the way over to the service. Mamí, who replaced the saints with *Fox's Book of Martyrs* a while back, says that all the thanks should go to God. They go out of the door, and I hear their Buick start up and head out our gravel driveway.

I am alone with God. That's about how it is for the next five years, working with the ladies on the Cherokee Reservation in North Carolina. I am alone with God. I mean, I see people, I visit the sick and afflicted. I lay the palms of my hands on them and they get better. People bow their heads when they walk by.

Voices carry, talking about how my prayers can change the weather. This is on account of the drought we had back home in Kentucky a couple of years back. I went outside, laid on the ground, and asked God to make it rain. Preachers from the Methodist Holiness Temple and the nuns from Sacred Heart of Jesus Convent did the same thing, I should add. Whether it was coincidence that it didn't start raining until I got up off the ground, I don't know. Anyway, that kind of carried the saint thing over this way.

That is, until I meet Bo Notices. That's his name. Like mine is Sao. The first time I meet him, he comes into the back of the Amazing Grace Pentecostal Holiness Church. The cinderblock church was built six months after I was born, by a teenage preacher who had seen it in a vision. Only has six members, so a general evangelist comes over from Cullowhee and preaches about working while it is day or abiding in Christ or the soon return of the Lord. It's always one of those three sermons. I sing and teach the Ladies' Bible Class.

So it's after that when Bo Notices wanders into the cool dark of the just-ended service. Everybody has had a handshake and sung *When We All Get to Heaven* and filed out the back door when he comes in. He surprises me and I drop all five copies of the *Broadman Hymnal*.

"I'm sorry," he smiles. "Bo Notices." He bends over and picks up the hymnals. The back of his wrist brushes my ankle. My breath catches in my throat.

"Notices what?" I ask.

He grins. His teeth are perfectly square, lined up like blocks in his head. "Notices. That's my name. My daddy's name. My granddaddy's name. But not my great-granddaddy's name."

He hands the hymn books back to me. I take them and put them on the second pew from the front, where Sally Rideout usually sits. A lady beetle is walking across that pew. Good thing Sally Rideout isn't here. She doesn't share her seat with anybody, man or beast.

"Why not your great-granddaddy's name?"

Bo Notices grins again. "His name got changed on the census. It was originally Notices-Rain, on account of my great-great-great-granddaddy could tell you to the minute when rain was on the way."

So can I, I think, but I keep that to myself. "Oh. Well, the preacher already left, Brother Notices." Notices-Rain, I want to say, but I remind myself that after the census, it just isn't that way anymore.

Bo Notices tilts his head and looks me in the eye, which makes me shy. " I didn't come to meet him. I want to meet God."

"God?"

"God. Folks around here seem to think that you know him pretty well. So I figured if I met you, you could at least tell me where to find Him."

"God?"

Bo Notices chuckles, low in his throat. "God."

"Well, it isn't like He's got a street address. You find God in the Bible—"

"I've heard all that," Bo Notices stops me. "I've even read the Bible—stole a Gideon one from a hotel in Texarkana. But I want to find God."

I'm calculating the possibility of finding God in a stolen Bible, when Bo Notices says something to me that nobody has ever said and probably never will say yet.

"There's something of God in the way you smile."

"What?" I can't recall ever seeing Bo Notices before, much less smiling at him.

He grins again. "I watch you. I've been watching you. You smile at people and they smile back like the Queen of England just complimented them on their dress. That's what made me think you might know where to find God."

"Well, I've got these tracts on 'The Four Steps to Salvation'—"

"No! No thank you. Not one more road map or manual or set of directions. I came to find out how to find God."

All of the sudden, I am not so sure that sainthood equips you for the job of evangelism. Bo Notices laces his fingers together, and begins to sing, "'Here is the church, here is the steeple, open the door and see all the people.' I know I can come to church or go practice yoga or something. But I don't want to *do* something and hope God shows up. I want to meet Him personally."

"I understand." And I do, too.

He sighs. "So what do you do?"

I shrug. I am glad that I wore my white sailor dress instead of the gray cotton dress that dips in the front. "I guess I just talk to Him. I just greet Him and talk to Him and He talks back. Just like a regular conversation. So far, He's always replied. He's never been rude yet."

Bo Notices' brows come together. Then he smiles, light all over his face. "Okay. Okay. Talk to Him and He talks back. Talk to Him and He talks back." He sticks out his hand, shakes mine. "Talk to Him and He talks back." Bo Notices repeats this as he strides out the church door.

I sit on the edge of Sally Rideout's pew. Talk to God and He talks back. I wish all of life was this easy.

I eat my wish seven days later. Bo Notices is sitting in the third pew on the left-hand side as the song service starts. He sings, off-key but heartily, along with *When the Roll is Called Up Yonder* and *What a Friend We Have in Jesus*—first, second, and last verses. We take up the offering and Bo Notices puts in fifty dollars—our biggest bill yet. After that, Sister Betty Spencer testifies for the Lord. So does Brother John Spencer. I don't expect anything else to happen, once the preacher starts to close the service.

Bo Notices stands up. "Excuse me," he says. "As far as I'm concerned, this woman here's a saint."

The word hits me somewhere I can't name. I've heard it all my life, but coming from Bo Notices, it's different.

"Ladies and Gentlemen of the church, I met God."

Everybody gasps. Evidently they know something about Bo Notices that he hasn't let me in on yet. Bo Notices grins at them, showing all of those wonderfully square teeth of his.

"Yes, I met God. Thanks to Miss Espiritu here, I went riding on my motorcycle. I stopped by the river and I said, "Hello, God. If You are there, I'd like to introduce myself. My name is Alphaeus Notices, but everybody calls me Bo."

I interrupt before I can help myself. "Alphaeus?"

"Yeah," Bo Notices replies.

I feel like I'm watching my life, rather than living it. "Where'd you get Bo?"

"*Dukes of Hazzard*." I nod. Bo Notices plunges forward into his testimony. "Anyway, I introduce myself to God. 'I think that it's about past time that we met,' I tell Him. 'I hope that we can talk and maybe get to be friends. I have done a lot of bad things and I'm sure that You've seen them or heard tell of them, but I'd like to mend my ways and be a better person. So if You'd like to talk to me, feel free at any time.'"

Sally Rideout looks at him, bug-eyed. "So, then what happened?"

"Nothing."

Everybody looks like you just let the air out of them. I can see their minds turning back to chicken and corn-bread and beans waiting on the stove. Bo Notices claps his hands together.

"At least not at first. I sat there and sat there and, finally, I figured that either God's not up there or He doesn't have anything much to say to me. So I get up, and as I throw my leg over my Harley, I hear 'A pleasure meeting you.' Just like I'd hear you. So I sit back down and talk to God and He talks back." Bo Notices gestures to me. "Just like you said He would."

Sister Gisgi turns toward me. "You told him God would talk to him?"

"Well, I . . . Yes, Ma'am. Why not?"

"Why him? He never says anything to me," Sally Rideout whines.

"I didn't mean to make it seem like God plays favorites," I venture, trying to make peace. "I think He'd probably talk to anybody."

"Obviously," says Jenna Rideout, Sally Rideout's former daughter-in-law. She used to be married to Sally Rideout's second son, Geronimo. It's a long story. And no, his given name isn't Geronimo. That's one thing about this part of the country, nobody is who they say they are.

"Well," Bo Notices says slowly, "I appreciate y'all's patience, and I just wanted you to know that I am a changed man. God talked to me and I aim to be His friend." He sits down. I rescue the service by singing *We're Marching to Zion*. I am glad when we all go home.

Home. That's one place where sainthood is truly important. I live in a trailer in back of the Amazing Grace Pentecostal Holiness Church. Pictures of flowers and sayings from the Psalms cover the walls. I am lonely, but that seems to be a prerequisite for sainthood. Church ladies bring me cobbler, dumplings, and chicken on Sundays, but they never invite me to eat with them. I figure it's one of them knocking on the door, three Sundays later.

I open the screen. Bo Notices waves at me.

"Hey," he says, "Wanna go riding?"

He has a Harley parked in front of my trailer—well, the church's trailer, really, they just let me use it. Now, I have never ridden on a motorcycle in my life. There's another thing I haven't done, and that's wear pants. Saints in slacks are frowned upon.

"I can't." I start to close the screen.

Bo Notices catches the door. "You won't get mangled, I promise."

"No, that's not it. It's just that I can't wear a dress on that thing." And that saints on motorcycles jeopardize their saintly status.

"I figured that." Bo Notices hands me a bag from Wal-Mart. I pull out what looks to be a skirt, only it isn't. "A skort," he explains. "Like pants, only you can pull the front part over and it looks like a skirt."

"Oh." I take the bag.

"Take your time," Bo Notices tells me, "I'll be waiting. Take all the time you need."

I turn around and enter the trailer. I try to hurry, only I can't. When I come out, I apologize for taking so long. I had to find some tights to go under the skort.

"It's alright. I told you to take your time. I told you I'd wait." Bo Notices smiles at me. I know he means every word.

The sun is setting when we return to the trailer. Going to bed early is another rule of sainthood. Work while it is day, rise and pray while it is yet night. I climb off the Harley, keeping my eyes on the ground.

"Thank you," I tell Bo Notices. "For all of it."

"You're welcome. You told me how to meet God. I figured the least I could do is take you riding."

Bo Notices rides away. I watch him until he becomes very small.

I cannot tell you how the rest happens. All I know is that Bo Notices and I go fishing and cook our fish in foil over the campfire. We go walking on trails that lead through dogwood and ferns. I do not know how I end up eating flan and hominy with Bo Notices. All I know is that I am placing dishes in the sink when I feel him behind me.

"Sao," he says. I have never heard him use my name before. "You are a beautiful woman."

I drop the silverware. Forks, knives, spoons, clatter against chrome.

"Missionary." The word slips out before I consider how much it will weigh.

"Woman. You were a woman before you were a missionary. And, as a man, I'm asking you to marry me."

I forget to remember to breathe. Bo Notices kisses the back of my neck. Slow and sweet, like he's leaving something there instead of taking it away. My knees give and I feel his arms around me, holding me up. "This is what

I'm going to do," he says against my earlobe, "I'm going to leave you be. All I ask is that you ask God if you should marry me."

All my thoughts are in broken, odd angles. "Fair enough."

"One thing extra," he whispers. I nod. It's about all I can do to do that. "Do whatever He says."

"Saints do not get married," Mamí says over the phone. "They are either already married, or they stay unmarried. They do not *get* married." She pulls out *Fox's Book of Martyrs* and slams it on her kitchen table. It sounds loud, even all these miles away.

"You are ruining all our plans," Papí adds, talking on the extension.

Things do not get any better outside my kitchen. I run into Sally Rideout at the market.

"I just think," she sneers, "that a Christian woman, such as yourself, should not be taking up with such a person as Bo Notices." She lowers her voice into a whisper that can probably be heard in Canada. "He's done *time*."

"We've all been convicted, Sister Rideout," I tell her. Her eyes widen. "Of sin, of doing wrong, that is. We just got saved so we don't have to pay for our sins."

Things get worse. The postman, the grocer, the funeral director, and every church lady who spots me takes the time to tell me the same things. Bo Notices drank. Bo Notices got a Caddo girl pregnant and she had an *operation*. Bo Notices was arrested for DUI. By the time they get through, I expect to hear that Bo Notices was born with horns and a tail.

Bo Notices and I are making supper in my trailer. I told Bo Notices how I heard that the Primitive Baptists used to drop the Bible on the floor and preach whatever it opened to. He suggests that we make supper the same way. We drop the Pentecostal Ladies' Circle cookbook (a fundraiser from 1942) on the floor, and it opens to "Decoration Day Dinner"—ham and pineapple, green beans, and egg salad. I don't eat pork, and Bo Notices doesn't like eggs, so we drop it again. This time, we fare better, with "South of the Border Supper"—tacos, refried beans, and green onions. We skip the onions, boil ears of corn instead. Bo Notices begins to sing *La Cucaracha* at the top of his lungs. Way out like we are in the middle of nowhere, no one can really hear us.

Except for the denominational elders at the front door. They clear their throats loudly as they knock on the door. It's their trailer. They could have just come in, but they knocked. Bo Notices stops singing. I smooth the sides of my chignon as I open the door.

"Hello, Sister Sao." The first elder and the second elder speak in unison, in the type of voice that is usually used for funeral homes. Jack Sprat could eat no fat, I think, since the first elder is spare and the second is stout. His wife could eat no lean. These men were young once, I think, and then I know they never were.

"Brethren." I open the screen and they come into the front room, where the kitchen blends into the space where Bo Notices stands.

The first elder straightens his tie. "Sister Sao, we are concerned . . . "

"Very concerned," the second elder chimes in.

"With Christian concern . . . "

"The concern of the Church . . . "

"About the company that you seem to be keeping . . . "

"With such a one do not eat . . . "

I sink into a kitchen chair as the door closes behind them. Hell, fire, fear, and God. Suddenly, I am very tired. Bo Notices puts his hand on my shoulder.

"Sao?"

"Yes. I'm sorry, Bo."

Bo Notices sits in the chair next to mine. It doesn't match and is higher above the table than my chair, which has one short leg.

"Don't be sorry. They're right, Sao. I was a rough customer. I drank, I fought, but I never did time. And that girl? She's got my child, married a Choctaw guy. I can't do anything about my life then, but I trust God to work in it now."

"God forgives," I start. Blood presses noisily against my head.

"I ain't worried about God," Bo Notices says. "I know He forgives. It's people that don't."

He reaches his hand across the table. "Listen, Sao, this is what I want to know. Just this one thing. Do you think, even for one second, that they might be right? That you might lose your salvation and go to Hell over me?" His eyes are large, pleading.

Who was it—Penelope, Hermione, the saint that refused to marry? Perpetua? My whisper comes out raw and verges on a sob. "I don't know."

Bo Notices nods. "Well, I won't cost you Heaven."

Once he rides away, the quiet is painful.

Alone is a state where you need an imagination. Mine wanders, focuses on Bede and Bernard of Clairvaux, makes stories of Saint Thomas, who spent a sultan's money building castles in Heaven. I think Joan of Arc made sense. I wish myself on the back of that Harley. Then I repent. I read all of the prophets. The Book of Nahum makes me cry.

Somewhere left of three in the morning, I hear a pounding on my trailer. Insistent. I stumble out of the bedroom as the front door opens. That's one thing about saints, to practice sufficient hospitality, you must never lock your doors.

"Sister Sao, come quick," Jenna Rideout pants. She looks peaked. Despite Pentecostal prohibitions, she must usually wear foundation makeup. "Geronimo's been in a bad accident. We need you to come lay hands on him so he'll live." Without her cosmetics, Jenna has freckles. She looks young and scared.

She drives me over to Baptist General. Pentecostals don't have hospitals on account of believing in divine healing and all. So in spite of our doctrinal differences, we appreciate the Baptists.

"Geronimo was driving. Drunk. He hit a tree. Bo Notices was passing by and went for an ambulance."

Bo Notices. The name pinches my heart. Hard.

When we pull up at the ER, we run in. Pretty much the entire congregation and quite a few Freewill Baptists— from Geronimo's daddy's side—await me.

"Oh, Sister Sao," Sally Rideout cries out, "go in there and heal my baby."

I step behind drawn curtains. Tubes and wires thread their way in and out of Geronimo Rideout's body. He gasps for air.

"Geronimo," I say, tasting the urgency. "There's no time to waste. I know you believe in Jesus, or you did when you were a little boy." Geronimo Rideout tries to nod.

"Now, Geronimo—" His breath wheezes, and I realize that he is trying to tell me something. I bend my head to hear his whisper. "Francis, I mean to say, Francis, you need to trust God right now. I mean, nobody can help you as much as He can. Will you trust Him?"

Francis Geronimo Rideout squeezes my hand.

"Alright then, just ask Jesus to save you."

Francis Geronimo Rideout breathes out three words, "Jesus, save me," before the monitor flatlines. Doctors and technicians fly to the bedside. They push me aside. The Rideout family passes me, shoving their way close to the curtained cubicle. I need to get some air.

"I heard what you did." The coal-colored face of the orderly behind me shines like the sky in Kentucky at night. "I think you're a saint."

The words sink in for a moment. "No," I tell him. "Not a saint. Not anymore. I don't think I ever was."

I walk through the electric doors of the emergency room. Bo Notices stands in the fire lane, waiting for me. He holds out his hand. I take it. No matter how they tell it, wax and plaster saints have nothing on flesh and blood.

What Passes for Wisdom

Sao Notices Knowing

I know my father is having an affair the same way I know everything else. I have a dream. Not a dream like when you wake up you know you've been dreaming, but a dream that's as real as real. I should say first that my dreams have never been quite like everyone else's. Mine have credits. And musical numbers. I dream in color, the type that appears in hand-tinted portraiture. My dreams rival MGM or Columbia Pictures' best work in every way but one—my dreams come to pass.

Papí and I are driving down Raccoon Gap Road. His old Buick, which is green and starts up no matter what the thermometer says, needs a new muffler.

"Papí, do you have a girlfriend?" I ask, just like that.

Papí presses his lips together. "Yes."

"Well," I answer. Then I turn around and look out the windshield. The trees are covered with snow, which falls from the branches as we drive by.

My shoulders shake. I am shivering. My husband, Bo, encircles me with his arms. I feel his heat entering my skin.

"I have to go back to Kentucky," I tell him. My teeth are chattering.

"We'll leave at sunrise," he whispers. I start to get warm.

I am not the least bit surprised to find my father's under-shirts hanging in the bushes. His socks are strewn across the grass. My mother and her sisters, Tía Verdella and Tía Vera are hurling my father's belongings into the front yard. His Sunday shirt covers the head of the rooster statue at the front steps.

Mamí and Papí have lived in this house for years—since it was red and white. Now, it has been sided with all-weather materials and high interest payments.

"Bo!" I shout, but my husband has already dodged whatever Mamí and her sisters have tossed out the window. Bo moves to my side at the front door.

"You'd best not come in, Beloved," I tell him, stopping to touch his cheek. "If they're this upset, seeing a man might not help."

Bo winks at me. "Not the man that deflowered a saint, anyway."

"You married me first," I smile back. "There are married saints." You are one, I think about my husband. My husband taught me about grace. Every Name of God I know, I know because of my husband's love. If this doesn't qualify him for sainthood, I don't know what does.

"I'll be right here," Bo says, walking back toward our Jeep. I love it when he says that. He will be.

Mamí and her sisters are swearing in a cross between Portuguese and Spanish.

"Mamí."

The swearing stops. They have not seen me since I left mission work to marry Bo Notices. They were not there. They do not take my calls.

My aunts stop throwing things. My mother looks me up and down.

"Well, you're not pregnant. There's still hope for an annulment."

"Mamí, I've been married five months. I am very much my husband's wife."

"Were you in your right mind? Were you married in the church?"

"I'm fine, Mamí. And we were married at Wright's Creek Baptist."

"Like Joan of Baptist."

"John the Baptist, Mamí. Joan of Arc."

"Ay! See, you remember your saints. There's hope for you still."

I sigh. This was my life, once, mending my parents' hearts.

"Mamí, I know about Papí."

"Well, then you know where he is. Go get him and bring him home."

If she wanted him to come home, why throw his belongings through the window? My parents make their own kind of sense. When they apply their particular wisdom, the rest of the world seems inside out. Lord, please have mercy. Make today the last time I rescue my parents.

"I don't know where Papí is, Mamí. I only dreamed what he's been doing."

The night before I married Bo Notices, I had a dream. I dreamed that I was riding in a lifeboat, when a storm came up. My mother and father were sinking in strong waves on my left side, while Bo was treading water on my right. Wearing a lifejacket, I held the only rope. All of them were calling my name. My mother cannot swim.

"He's at the Mays' house," Mamí interrupts my musings. "You know, that no-'count Mays whose brother used to be sheriff for so long?"

"His daughter came back from heaven-knows-where after her daddy died," Tía Vera picks up the conversation. Tía Verdella is tossing Daddy's El Toro aftershave gift set out the window. My life has gone from nothing missing, nothing broken, to a cartoon, all in a matter of miles.

"Don't even bother coming back without your father," declares Mamí.

"Alright, Mamí." I turn to leave.

"Sao?"

"Yes, Mamí?"

"When you get back, we can go see Father Guerra about that annulment."

I threw the rope to Bo. When he grins at me from the driver's side of our Jeep, I feel absolved for letting my parents drown.

The Mays' house is pitiful, the kind of place Americans like to think can only happen overseas or across the border. I knock. Twice.

"Come on in."

I do. A television set is the only light. I start toward it, making my way through a haze of smoke and dust.

A girl sits on the sofa. An afghan covers it, one of those that somebody's grandmother or great-aunt made. Who grows up to make afghans? Probably the same kind of girl that grows up to be a saint. The girl's hair is dry, with bangs across her forehead. I squint through her cigarette smoke.

"Do you remember me, Sao?"

I don't and then I do. Not her, the dog on the rag rug beside her.

"I remember Cumberland," I tell her.

She smiles. Her teeth are yellowed and crooked. Well water, I think. Sulphur.

"Cumberland," she repeats, as if hearing it for the first time. "I can't believe you recall his name."

I reach over and pat the dog on his side. He blinks at me through rheumy eyes. Eyes like that on a dog always hurt my feelings. The glaze over the cornea means the end is coming.

"Hello, Cumberland."

The girl coughs. "All these years and you remember his name."

"You remember mine."

She nods. "You got God to heal my dog. How could I forget? All this time I keep thinking about you . . . He . . . " She starts to swear and reconsiders, as most people do around me. "Most days I wish I was you."

Not today, you don't, I think. You don't hardly wish that you were talking to the woman who's committing adultery with your father.

She coughs again. Her nose runs and she wipes it with the back of her hand. I reach into my pocketbook and hand her a napkin from Charro's Tacquería. When she takes it, I notice her nails. Chewed, bitten deep into the cuticle. Tormented. That's the word I'm looking for. When I find it, it fits the entire situation. "Look . . . "

"Lena, my name is Lena."

"Alright, Lena. I'm not here on a social call. I'm here to retrieve my father and take him home to my mother."

"Juan is your father?"

"And my mother's husband."

Her hand shakes as she lights another cigarette. "What do they say, an eye for an eye? If I say no, are you going to take back Cumberland?"

Camels. Unfiltered. I want Bo. He stayed in the Jeep, in case we needed to make ourselves a quick getaway. One thing about Bo, he's not much on miracles. He says he'd rather be alright with God all the time than to get so desperate that he needs the whole Holy Trinity to get him out. Right about now, I think Bo has a good point.

"No. It doesn't work like that. God wants everyone to win. You don't win, Lena, not like this. I mean, maybe you think you love my father and maybe you do, but the truth is still that he isn't yours to love. And so I don't have to do anything. Neither does God. The two of you curse yourselves by walking out from under where He can bless you."

Lena blinks at me. Red lines curve over her eyeballs. Her voice breaks. "Nobody ever loved me besides your daddy and Cumberland."

"Nobody loved me either, Lena. They loved the miracles God let me do, loved what I knew or could do for them. But I did the right thing, even when it didn't look like it worked. And then one day, when I thought that I would never be happy, nothing would ever go right, I just made an announcement to God that, no matter what, I would do the right thing for the rest of my life."

Lena looks up at me. "What happened then?"

"Nothing. Not for a while. And then just when I got used to being miserable, God surprised me. I got married."

The tears in Lena's eyes startle me. "Are you happy?"

"Very."

"Then listen to me," Lena blows a smoke ring into the air. "You did me a favor once, so I'll do you one now. Walk out that door and go home to your husband. Whether I stay seeing Juan or not, you need to know that you're the one it'll cost. If you put your family back together, you're gonna be the glue that keeps it together. And that'll cost you everything that makes you so happy."

"My mother—"

Lena interrupts. "I'm sure. I mean what I say. Unless you want to spend the rest of your life in Nowhere, Kentucky, keeping tabs on Juan, you'd best turn right around and go back to your happiness." She inhales again and releases a puff of smoke. "And no matter what you see, no matter what you hear—in spite of what you think you know—stay where you're happy and don't let anything drag you away."

"Baby."

I hear my father's voice from the back of the house. Sluggish, sleepy, as if he's been drunk.

"Baby, who's there?"

"Ain't nobody." Lena stands up, picks up her lighter and her ashtray. As she leaves the room, she whispers, "You go on and be happy."

My father's low laugh slides under her raucous one. Maybe Lena Mays knows something I don't. Cumberland whines. I pass my hand over his aging eyes, and ask God to do me a favor. He does.

"Bye, Cumberland," I tell him. Wagging his tail, he looks at me through clear lenses.

As Bo drives our Jeep down the gravel driveway, my hands claw at my sweater, at the smell of smoke.

"Bo . . . "

My husband turns his head. He turns onto the dirt road, the only way back to the main road.

"I can't go back to Mamí's. Take me out of here. I can't stand these clothes. Bo . . . "

My husband looks at me again, and concern shadows his face. He pulls our Jeep off the road into a thicket of trees. His hands move over buttons and against zippers, into water and salt, far away from what passes for wisdom.

Wont to Haunt

Lena Allen Mays Changing

This is what I do. I come out of the back bedroom and open up a can of jack mackerel for Cumberland. Me, I can't stand the stuff, but Cumberland's gotten a taste for it in his old age. When I put it into his dish, I stir in a raw egg. I call him twice, like usual. He gets up and walks across the floor, like usual, only not.

Cumberland can see. Usually he sniffs his way over to his food, on account of his eyes are kindly poor and he can't see as good as before. Well, this time he doesn't sniff. He just comes over and starts to eating.

God has done Cumberland another miracle. Chill bumps rise at the base of my spine and chase each other up into the nape of my neck. Sao prayed for Cumberland. I'm sure she did. I mean, I didn't see it, but I know it. Kind of like you can't see Christmas, but you know it's either in front of or behind you all the time. Sao asked God to help Cumberland. Even knowing that I've been laying with her daddy. Even after I about told her to cut it out and leave.

"Cumberland," I call him. "Look at me, Cumberland. Here, look at me in the eyes." Cumberland raises his head. His eyes are clear and moist, like when we first left here and before we came back.

"I'll be . . . " I try to think of something to say I'll be. Cussing seems real inappropriate in the middle of a miracle. Besides, I don't think we are what I thought we were. I think we just got helped.

Us. Cigarette smoke swirling all around us, and somebody else's husband back there in the bed. Troubled as we can be, and God gave us a miracle.

"We are not living like this no more, Cumberland," I tell him. His head tilts to the side for a moment, then returns to the middle. "I mean it." I do, too. Glass clangs against glass as I push beer bottles into the wastebasket. Marching into the front room, I pick up the plastic ashtrays and several packs of cigarettes. I crush up the cigarettes and toss them and the ashtrays in with the bottles.

"No more. Not for us." I walk out the front door and set the whole mess on the curb. Juan calls me everything but for supper when I tell him to leave. I lock the door behind him, that's how much I don't care. I don't even want these sheets anymore, and they're the only set Mama had that matched. I ball them up and toss them into the back yard.

There's a phone book by the bed. Every church in three counties with a phone is listed. Then it comes to my mind that maybe the best ones don't even have a phone line. Maybe those are the ones that hear from Jesus directly.

"We are going to get back in church, Cumberland." I make myself laugh, saying that out loud. Truth is, we were never in church. Closest to church we ever got was once, years ago, when Marthal, Jimmy's wife, took us to Vacation Bible School over at the Holiness Temple. I can't call his name, but the pastor patted Cumberland and let him come on in to the classroom. Said he could see how Cumberland was an extra special dog and how he would behave himself in Vacation Bible School. The next day, the pastor's wife baked cookies for the children, and she even made one without sugar for Cumberland. I think about that cookie for a minute, and I know where we should go.

The way I feel now, I don't care what's going on. I'll sit in a funeral, a wedding, whatever's going on at the church. I just want to get to know God.

"I'll be right out, Cumberland," I tell him as I turn on the shower. The handles have been broken off for years and you have to turn what's left of the knobs with a screwdriver. That's one thing I'm going to do after I get back from the church, is get this house together. This place is no kind of home for me and Cumberland in our new lives.

"Just you wait and see, Cumberland," I holler. "Things are gonna be set right around here."

I step into the shower. I turn up the water as hot as I can stand and let it run all over me. I imagine it washing away all I ever did wrong.

The Color of Blood

Lena Allen Mays Leaving

"You want to be different, you got to go somewhere different."

That's what I tell Cumberland as I put the shopping bags full of our lives into the back of Daddy's old truck. It used to be Ray Allen's and Daddy's together, until Ray Allen took pity on Daddy and paid it all the way off. I was gone then, bringing drinks to casino tables and doing whatever I could to get by. The way I feel now, I don't even know myself doing that. I mean, I know I must have been like that, but it's like watching a movie where somebody plays me. I recognize my life, but I don't remember living it.

That's why me and Cumberland are leaving. You know that old saying about how home is where the heart is? Well, it's also where your reputation is. People always trying to know you, not letting you change. Folks like that might as well go on ahead and call God a liar to His face, saying He can make a world in a week and then acting like He can't change a plain old human person overnight.

At least that's what I think. I'm coming out of the Holiness Temple, which I can truly say has some fine people in it. This I know, because Cumberland sat out in the hallway between the front door and the sanctuary and just about every saint stopped on the way out and petted his head. And they all shook my hand and told me about how glad they were that I was on some narrow path and that if I stayed on it, I'd get to Heaven. No, the saints aren't the trouble with Cast Salt, Kentucky.

It's the sometimey saints that are the problem. You know the kind I'm talking on—the ones that ain't saints, they just wish they were. Maeline Jacks is like that. I'm walking out to the truck, and she's sitting out there in her mama's old Ford waiting on her. She ain't been to service in a year of Sundays, but she's picking up her mama and her mama's little mama, who is bent like you'd bend a paper clip.

"Well, look who the cat drug in," Maeline starts.

"Actually, Maeline, it's more like look who the Holy Ghost is working over," I correct her. I am trying my best to be sweet, now that I have religion and all.

She snorts through her nose. "I guess He really meant that about whosoever," she says, smarty-like.

I feel generous, since I have had such a good time in church. "Well, then we certainly both qualify."

When I drive away, I lean over to Cumberland. "I am amazed at me, Cumberland. I am entirely a different sort of person."

I am, too. Unfortunately, Ricky Ricklin can't see the transformation. He hollers out the window of his Camero. Calling me like I'd take up with some trashy, good-for-nothing like him. Instead of hollering around, I make myself think charitable thoughts on account of his wayward living and Hell-bound destination.

When I pull up in front of Daddy's old house, its sagging roof and papered windows startle me. This is where we lived. This is who we were.

"Cumberland, we need to be where we belong."

Everybody and his cousin heads up North. They do. Made Kentucky the biggest state in the Union. Yes, sir. West Virginia? Kentucky part two. Indiana? Kentucky annex. And Southern Ohio might as well cooperate and change its name. Don't believe me? Watch the roads on weekends. Friday night, by five after five, I-71 and I-75 South got car after car all the way to Kentucky. Sunday night? Them same folks wrap up pintos and cornbread from supper and head back up to work.

Me and Cumberland have creativity. We are going further down South. Funny thing is, it's Mama who decides it. As soon as we get back from service at the Holiness Temple, I grab me a plastic bag.

"Snatch and run, Cumberland." Cumberland pads over to the front door and waits. He's got that right. The whole lot of nothing left in this house isn't worth us worrying over. We should probably just get in the truck and head on out.

"You know what to say, Cumberland," I tell him, "but I want to poke around and see if there's anything we can use."

Well, I open my closet and realize something. I don't even like my clothes anymore. They look like they belong to somebody else, which in a way they do.

That's why I go in Mama's closet. Her dresses are longer, cover more and cover better. Sliding them off the hangers, I fold them into my grocery bag. Two pairs of shoes sit on the floor, but I decide against taking them. I think about something I learned when I went to visit Girl Scouts with my cousin Denise, back in the third grade. Something about walking in somebody else's moccasins. My mama's shoes are nice, but I sure don't want her life.

I look up at the two shelves in the closet. The lowest one is empty, except for dust. I pull a chair over. It looks like it will hold me, so I stand on it. Then I reach into the unknown.

A cigar box sits at the back of the top shelf. Three Dutchmen in frilly collars sit on the front of the box. Frozen. I lift the lid. It ain't my business, but it is. The box is probably like the rest of this house, filled with things that ain't mattered since a long time ago.

I am about right, pushing past ticket stubs and matchbooks, until I open a vanilla envelope. No label or nothing, just a picture of four girls, sitting on the front porch of a saltbox house. You know how they say "pretty as a picture"? That's how these girls are, smiling at somebody I can't see.

I forget to remember to breathe at the next one. My heart beats twice in the same time it's supposed to beat once. The man in the picture is some kind of wonderful. Tall, with teeth that jump right out of his dark face. He is wearing a big cowboy hat. A giant buckle divides his body into halves.

I turn the pictures over. "Who are you?" I wonder if Mama loved this man—well, she must of to have kept his picture all this time. And these girls. I look at them again. The one on the left end looks like the mannequins they used to have in Ward's, before it closed down and before these other stores got bodies without faces, sometimes without heads. Her face is perfect, and her eyes are the kind of sweet I've seen before but can't place. But it's the one in the middle I keep coming back to. Her face is entirely round. Round eyes, round face, round cheeks, even her lips are circles set in line. If the one on the left is a beauty, this one looks like a Saint Valentine's Day angel. All of the sudden, right as I look at the picture, her face narrows, and all the round goes out. Under this smiley face is Mama's.

"Mama?" I ask the black and white figures. "Oh, Mama." All at once, I know that Mama was happy, and I wish that I had met her then. It is the strangest thing, how our parents used to be real people before we happened to them.

"Mama? Who were you?" As soon as I say this, I get my answer. A white piece of paper tucked in the envelope talks back. Certificate of Live Birth. Georgia Stands-Straight. Mama's first name was Georgia, but her last name was Smith. That's what Daddy always said. Smith. As ordinary as butter or salt, flour or lard. But the dates match up. Oklahoma Redpaint Standstraight. Mama has a mama. Of course, everybody does, but my mama has a mama with a name. And a daddy. Jack. But it's the next line that bites my tongue.

We are Colored. Me and Mama. Cherokee Indian.

No need to wonder why Mama hid this. Just Daddy and his narrow mind could have kept her quiet. The news makes me feel better, like we ain't as much kin to Daddy and his trashy ways as it seemed. I mean, I don't know much beyond late-night Westerns about Indians, but they—I guess *we* now—seem to have gotten a bad deal.

Kentucky ain't exactly a place to be Colored of any kind. I feel in danger now, like everything I recognize just turned on me. But I turn it over again, and know I didn't need any of it anymore, anyway.

I look back to the pictures. "Nice to meet you, Mama," I tell her. My eyes pass over the girl on the left, who looks like a movie star. All of the sudden, I know those eyes. The ones on the prettiest girl. She's got eyes like Sao, clear and peaceful, and I know where me and Cumberland got to go.

Butter and Honey

Sao Notices Hearing

My husband's body moves over mine when I hear it. I raise my hands instinctively to push him away. Bo Notices catches them both in his left hand. The beginning of tomorrow glints off his wedding ring.

"I heard it Sao," his hips slow as he presses his lips against my ear. "I heard it. It's alright."

"I don't . . . I can't," My answer catches in my throat and turns into tears. Bo Notices folds his fingers over mine. I hold on, counting them over and over again, as Bo Notices finds the rhythm that will make us a son.

Continual Coming

Lena Allen Mays Needing

What time it is was never made my life a lick of difference. Four o'clock in the morning, four o'clock in the evening, my life was the same. Only when I drive past other peoples' houses do I think that time matters. People with steady fathers start keeping an eye on the road around five. Mothers who make their children mind look out for school buses around 3:30. Mothers with kids on the short bus start watching an hour before. They have to stand out there to meet it.

If you have a family, every light in the house is on by sunset. Apartment complexes hurt my feelings, because lights are only on in one room at a time. You just know the person that lives there can hardly wait for the day when they have enough loved ones to run up a decent-sized electric bill.

Cumberland and I drive all day toward the reservation. We stop at a rest stop for Cumberland to do his business and then at the Dixie Stop Truck Plaza for me to get some gas. We don't have hardly any money. I explain this toward the sky, in the general direction of God, who does us a great big favor. We fill the tank once and run the rest of the way on fumes. We stop one more time, at a rest stop in Tennessee. Cumberland is associating with a dog from Florida, so I walk past the vending machines. Hungry. My belly thinks my throat's been cut, that's how bad it is.

"Gussie Dukes." I hear a quivering voice behind me. A Colored lady, about the shade of brown on top of good biscuits, reflects in the machine, over rows of snack cakes and crunchy chips. Wire glasses circle her eyes, which are big and set close together.

"Ma'am?" I turn around.

"Gussie Dukes," she steps toward me. Even on her pointed shoes, she only reaches my shoulder.

I smile at her, "Lena Mays."

"Lena. That's a pretty name."

"Yes, Ma'am.

"Ever heard of Lena Horne?"

I nod. "Yes, Ma'am. I sure have. My uncle called my name after her. She sure was pretty."

Miss Dukes' head jerks under her black-and-gray wig. "You know what to say! Never was anything before or since half as sweet as Lena Horne." She pauses for a moment, her little head bobbing in thought. "Except maybe Fredi Washington."

"I don't know who that is." Times like this, I wish I'd gone to school enough for it to stick.

"Well!" Miss Dukes shakes her head at me. She points toward the snack machine. "You lose your money?"

"No, Ma'am." Shame sticks in my throat for a moment. My mouth waters like when you know you have to upchuck and there's no way around it. "Didn't put any in. Didn't have any to put in."

"Oh." She nods like she knows. "Come on out to the car with me." Without waiting for me to answer, she turns and totters out toward a Lincoln Town Car. Black and just a-shining—four doors and everything.

"Look here, Dukes," she says into the open window. A cinnamon-brown man turns his head toward the sound of her voice. Dark glasses hide his eyes. I never understand that—why blind people wear sunglasses. Sunglasses are supposed to keep the sun from hurting eyes that can see it all too well. Don't know what they'd do for eyes that can't make out the distinction between night and day. I guess they are for the rest of us, to let us know before we say the wrong thing or run them out the crosswalk or something.

"We got us some company," Miss Dukes chirps. "Miss Lena . . . "

"Lena Mays," I offer quickly.

Miss Dukes takes up right where she left off making the introductions. "Miss Lena Mays, from . . . "

I push my hair behind my ears, like it matters. I always wonder if blind people know more than they let on. Like if they see some other way and end up knowing more than they're telling.

"Kentucky."

"Miss Lena Mays from Kentucky. Called Lena after Lena Horne."

"Is that a fact?" The Colored man nods like he can see me.

"She's white, though," Miss Dukes explains.

Now if I live 'til Jesus comes again, I won't never be ready to explain what I say next. Especially not raised up by Daddy, who'd have smacked my mouth for it.

"No, Ma'am, I'm not."

One second, I'm looking at Miss Dukes' wig. The next, her eyes are on mine, she turns her little head that fast.

"You're not?"

"No, Ma'am. I'm Colored, too. Cherokee Indian."

"Isn't that something?" Mr. Dukes replies, "My folks were part Chickasaw."

"Well. Well. My daddy and mama were both part Choctaw," Miss Dukes chimes in.

"Is that some kind of Indian?"

Miss Dukes grins at me. "Yes, sure is."

"Maybe we're some kind of kin or something." I need me a book about Indians. I didn't know there were all these different kinds.

All of the sudden, I realize that I might have all kinds of kin in all kinds of places, and not just white folks, either. The idea makes me happy, like me and Cumberland have somebody besides Daddy's people and their sorriness.

Miss Dukes looks me up and down. Mr. Dukes sits real still, like Mama used to. Maybe this is an Indian thing.

"Miss Lena, we have some cornbread and chicken. Would you like to have some?" The way Mr. Dukes says this, I feel like I've been invited to something bigger than supper. You couldn't make me feel more special if you had me as a guest on one of my talk programs.

"Sure would, Sir. Sure would."

Miss Dukes opens the driver side door and slides in. For a minute, I think they could put this in the funny papers, this itty-bitty lady driving around in this big old car. Me sliding into the backseat behind her.

"Just reach right into that basket there and help yourself. We already ate."

I open the lid of a woven basket and pull out a drumstick and a piece of cornbread. I sit right there and start eating.

"Aren't you going to ask the blessing?" Miss Dukes looks at me in her mirror.

She's right and I know it, but I might as well call up and make a person-to-person call to the President of these United States as talk to God.

"I don't know how," I confess. The first step is admitting you have a problem.

"Have you been saved?" Miss Dukes looks back in that mirror again.

"Yes!" I'm glad to say that. "I got back in church this week."

They smile together, like Mr. Dukes can see.

"And you don't know how to talk to God?" Miss Dukes sounds surprised.

"I thought that was for preachers," I tell her.

Mr. Dukes shifts around in his seat to face me. "Talking to God is like talking to your father."

Well, that settles that. Daddy tore his pants with me long time ago. I throw my hands in the air. "I never had too much use for my father, Sir. He stayed drunk . . . " My eyes sting. I wipe them on my sleeve.

"Imagine the very best father you can," Mr. Dukes says, trying again. "A father who never drinks or beats on his wife and kids. A father who takes his family to church and out to eat. A father who will never go out on his wife or leave his children behind. Now picture it's that father that gave you that food and say thanks to him."

My tongue swells against sobs. I put my whole face in my sleeve and bawl. When I finish, my nose is running. Miss Dukes hands me a paper napkin.

"Mr. Dukes, how do I say all that I'm feeling to God?"

Mr. Dukes tilts his head to the left. Maybe he's hearing something I can't.

"Miss Lena, I think that's what you just did."

Maybe it's just me, but nothing then or now tastes as good as that chicken and cornbread. They let me scrape all the bones for Cumberland.

I shake their hands as I get out of the car. Miss Dukes motions me down toward the window. She whispers in my ear, and her words smell of denture paste and lilacs.

"It's African American. Only backward folks still say Colored. And how I hear it, they say Native American now."

I nod, grateful not to be going into my new life talking ignorant. As they shift into reverse, I wave at them. I alternate hollering "Thank You" and "Goodbye" until they pull away and merge onto the highway and are all the way gone.

Midnight Loaves

Lena Allen Mays Knocking

"Hello, Cumberland," Sao says, just that calmly, like dogs just drive themselves up her road and knock right on her door on a daily basis. Cumberland wags his tail. He always has been one for acting gentlemanly.

"Won't you come in?" Sao opens the screen and Cumberland waltzes right in like he owns the place. She starts to shut the wood door behind them. I am amazed. This is a person who must believe in the impossible, like Cumberland really did make it all the way from Kentucky on his own. Wonder if she thinks he walked or rode.

I leap onto the porch. That is really something. Sao's house has a real front porch, not just a step or a stoop. A real porch. If I had something like this, there's no way you'd keep me inside.

"I drove Cumberland," I tell her. "I mean, I've never heard tell of a dog that could drive. Leastways, not on the four-lane."

Sao nods, taking the whole thing for serious. Her eyes—those clear, clean eyes—never change.

"I am straight-out sorry for what I done to your daddy. Your mama, really. There wasn't no right in it, and I'm sorrier than I can say. But I am a completely new person now. I got religion, and I aim to have it even better, like you do."

Sao tilts her head. "I don't have religion," she says, "but I know God."

"Well." I say it just like that. "Well." I never thought of that before, that you could know God like I know Cumberland or Marthal or whoever.

"Sao, I've hurt people and I've done bad things, and I am as sorry as I know how to be. I'll tell anybody. I know you know God. That's why I'm here—me and Cumberland. God's sure to come around to see about you, and maybe I can get to know Him, too."

Sao stands still in the doorway. She is picture-pretty, half her face lit by porchlight and the other half yet in the dark. No wonder God loves her.

"Bo," she calls over her shoulder, "Bo."

I half expect whoever Bo is to come throw me out in the road.

A man walks out of the lit front room into the hallway. Just seeing Sao, he starts grinning at her, and she smiles back like them two got a secret.

"What, dearest?"

My heart hurts like you knocked the wind out of me. Dearest. The way he says it, he ain't just flapping his gums, either. Nobody ever loved me except Jesus and Cumberland. I think that, then feel bad that them two ain't enough.

"Bo, darling, please roll out the sofa bed. We have a guest for the night."

"Sure, Honey," he says. He don't even look at me, just her. I bet they don't have a TV or pictures on the walls or anything, just sit and look at each other like art.

Sao opens the door. "Come in."

I step into the hallway. Cumberland is lying asleep, on the rug. My feelings smart a little that he didn't wait to sleep near me.

"He's tired," I try to explain away Cumberland's bad manners.

"So, are you, I'd imagine."

I am, in more ways than I can name. I stick out my hand toward Sao. She takes it. Her hand is tiny, and not one nail is chipped or bitten. Dishes and cigarettes have settled into mine.

"Thank you, Sao."

"For what?"

"For letting us in."

Those eyes smile along with her teeth. "You're welcome," she says, and I know we are.

Angelphilia

Sao Notices Practicing Hospitality

Unaware,
Entertain,
Offer oatmeal,
Invite them by name,
Open the door,
Let them in,
Spin
Yarns
Into robes,
Clothes
Suitable for sitting on the head of a pin.
Mix
Milk, eggs, flour,
Sour
Cream.
Stir in
Coriander seed.
Do not mind when they prefer commodity cheese.

The Weight of the Brass

Lena Allen Mays Learning

"My mamí used to call it a monkey puzzle." Sao shakes her hands over the sink. I'll swea—I'll swan if the drops don't just fall straight down the drain, I don't know what they done. She reaches up and wipes her hands on towels with embroidery on them. *A* is for apple, says one. *C* is for Cat is sewn on the other.

"What's *B* for?" I blurt out.

Sao smiles over her shoulder. "Baby."

"Oh." I should have known it'd be something wholesome like that. "What's a monkey puzzle?"

Sao picks up the bowl of wet snap beans. She carries it to the kitchen table and sits across from me. I am peeling potatoes. I am real good with a knife, I'll tell you. Mama never would touch one, on account of if she cut herself, she bled for days. Daddy stayed drunk, couldn't be trusted round nothing sharper than a pencil.

"Help me, Jesus." I say this out loud, before I have time to think.

"Amen," says Sao.

Her little hands snap the ends from the beans quick, making sharp sounds like a cap gun. Her red nail polish looks like Christmas against the green beans.

"What's a monkey puzzle? My mama used to say that, too."

Sao stops for a moment and sighs. "I'm not sure exactly. My mamí used to pray with a lady, Sister Carolyn Landers, who came over from Ohio. She must have said it around Mamí, since Mamí started saying it to me. She'd come in from working, take one look around the house and say it looked like a monkey puzzle. Near as I can figure, it's a great big mess."

"Well, that's me."

Sao shakes her head slowly from side to side. "No, that's your life. There's a difference."

"There is?"

"Has to be. You're alright, Sister Lena."

That's Sao all over. She calls everybody Sister this or Brother so-and-so. Well, almost everybody. Her husband, she just calls Bo.

"It's your life that needs a makeover."

I like that. I like thinking like my life could be done over again with a good concealer and some shading.

"Do you ever get tired? I ask.

"Of what?"

"Of being you. I mean, you ever think about just packing up and starting all over?"

Sao shakes her head again. "No. You do that, you just take yourself with you. Besides, you take pieces of other people with you."

At this exact moment, her husband, Bo, walks in. I mean, if I was writing a Hollywood movie, I would have timed it just like it happens. He walks in the back door and kisses her on top of her head. Sao turns her pretty face upward and he kisses her on the mouth. Not just like a little sorry peck either, but like he's been thirsty all day and the only thing he wants to drink is her.

"You're home early."

"We got done laying brick earlier than I expected."

"Do you always come straight home?" I ask before I think about it, then I feel ignorant for interrupting. After all, he has for the month that I've been here.

Bo looks at me like I just announced that I came from space. "Where else would I go?"

He turns to Sao. "Gil asked me about a job over in Hickory. Pays plenty more an hour."

Sao nods. "What'd you tell him?"

Bo shrugs. "Almost yes, until he said we'd have to stay over. I told him I didn't want to be away from you."

"What about the money?" One of these days, I will learn to keep my mouth shut.

"God has money," Sao answers.

"Love is harder to come by," Bo says.

He takes Sao by the hand and up the stairs. They leave me setting there with snap beans, potatoes, and no earthly idea what they mean.

Vanity and Vexation

Lena Allen Mays Trying

The first place I get work, it's a craft shop. Only it doesn't stay open all the time, and it doesn't need as many workers in cool weather as it does in hot. The days I work there, I unpack cardboard boxes and set stock out on the shelves. Boxes from China and Japan, by way of Knoxville and Atlanta. Ropes and ropes and ropes of bright glass beads, wound round into daisy chains and strung long into necklaces. Chicken feathers, dyed with neon colors, stuck on plastic strips with elastic around the back. Plastic, popeyed babies, grinning under scrap leather and squirrel fur, a dab of red paint filling the middle of their open mouths. All of it marked "Made in China" or "Made in Japan," big as day. The customers don't seem to pay it no mind. I guess people just don't see what don't suit their dreams.

People come in and out all day. I guess maybe because I'm out in the store, or maybe because when I stock a shelf, I have to stay in one place for more than a minute, people tend to talk to me. At me, I should say, since they hardly wait for me to answer back.

Most of them, they tell me stories. One lady walked right over and started telling me that her grandmother was the daughter of a chief, a real princess. I told her my mother's people weren't anything special or Mama wouldn't have ended up married to Daddy and his sorry situation. Being married to trash gave Mama the status of trash. From the pictures, Mama's people maybe might have been somebody.

The woman folded her face at me and made an "oh-h-h" type noise that let me know that she was truly sorry that I hadn't been born royal or something. She flipped her blond hair at me and said that she and her husband had started their own sweat lodge and I would be welcome anytime.

After she left, I told Nola what she said. Nola snorted, laughed until she started hacking.

"What's funny?"

"People. These people that come in, they all have royal blood. And that's nothing on the ones that say that they had a dream or that an eagle visited them and they just *knew* that they were Indian. Nobody wants to say that they had a great-great grandmother who carried water or slept around at the fort or was just a real, live woman who did the best she could do not to get carried off by a panther or eaten up with smallpox. They've all got princesses hidden in the family closet."

I don't say anything, since the closet is just where I found out that my mama was Cherokee Indian.

Nola's wound up tight now and sputters. "And you leave them sweats alone. That's from out the Plains. Cherokee ain't supposed to sweat."

"So, what do most Cherokee do to pray?"

Nola winks at me. "Girl, you see all these churches around here?"

I get to thinking that there is a large tribe of people I don't know about. The "Wannabe" tribe. People are all the time calling somebody that. One Wednesday, a lady with hair the color of *I Love Lucy*'s comes in looking for a "tear" dress. I ask her what that means, and she tells me it's the Cherokee people's traditional dress. I make me a mental note to read up on these things. No scissors, she says, but every piece is torn out of the cloth by hand, without patterns. That sounds hard to me. I never did like home-economics class, on account of no guys. And 4-H was for girls that had mothers.

"Do you have one or not?"

"No Ma'am. We've got moccasins, though. Hard sole, soft sole, all different kinds."

"Those I bought at the Gathering of Nations," she tells me. I need an authentic tear dress."

"Are you Cherokee?" I blurt that out without thinking. It's that red, red hair.

Funny thing about it, we don't even know how red Lucy's hair was, on account of the shows were on black-and-white TV. We just take everybody's word for it. Well, that and publicity photos.

"In part," she answers.

I stop myself before I ask what part. That's so stupid, the way people ask if you are part Indian, like you should say, "Why yes, my left leg or my kidneys or the right quarter of my body," in reply. Nobody does that to any other group of people on the planet. Where I come from, if you walked up to somebody and asked, "Is your left arm Irish?" they'd knock you out.

"Last autumn, I went to a powwow in honor of the elders. The MC announced a very special ceremony in which he asked certain of us to come into the circle. There, we danced around, and then he announced that we were members, officially, of the Wannabe tribe."

"I've heard a lot about them," I say, silently counting the beaded, silver, and turquoise bracelets on her left arm.

Nola's dry laugh crosses the shelves. Sixteen. After the redhead walks out, I ask Nola about the Wannabe tribe.

"Get hooked on phonics," she cackles, "Sound it out."

Other customers, they start with a question, like "Are these authentic chief headdresses?"—as if they would be for a dollar and a quarter—or "Did real Indians make these?" and go from there. I asked my boss, Nola, if I should answer that particular one or not. She laughed and took a long drag on her cigarette.

"See those skirts over there?" I follow the orange at the end of her cigarette in the direction of patterned cotton. They are the kinds of things I think of hippies wearing—people who want to look like they have a culture, but aren't too sure what it is.

"Yeah," I nod. I should have said, "Yes, Ma'am." I try to remember for next time.

Nola winks at me. "*Those* were made in India. By Indians." In marketing, geography is important once in a while.

Nola is exactly the kind of person I could see myself being, if I hadn't made steps to improve my life. That's why I like her but am a little afraid of her at the same time. I know all it would take is one more pack of cigarettes, another woman's husband, or a twelve-pack of something I know better than to name, to set me back on the path I was on. The path Nola is finishing out. I mean, I like Nola well enough to worry about her, especially when her chest shakes with coughing and brings up strings of green, and I appreciate her giving me this job more than I can tell. But there's one thing that makes me know I can't grow up to be Nola, whatever it takes. Her laugh.

Nola laughs hollow, like there's nothing behind it. Me and Cumberland never had much to laugh about, and my mama never laughed—not that I remember. Daddy only laughed when he was drunk or telling tales to Ray Allen or wanting a woman. So that ain't a good guide to genuine laughter. And, now that I think about it, I wouldn't even bring it up or have given it too much of my thoughts until I heard Sao laugh. Like somebody tickled a little girl or threw her into the air and caught her again. Just from being glad to be alright all the time. Laugh like that, there's no meanness in it.

I walked into the front room after work Tuesday before last, and there were Bo and Sao, setting over in Bo's recliner. I say setting, but it was more like laying, really. She was on his lap, which made sense, since don't nobody sit in that big chair but Bo. I mean, he loves Sao to death, would do anything for her, give her anything he had, but even she doesn't go near that chair. Big as Bo is, Sao sitting on him was like sitting in a whole 'nother chair. Both of them were about asleep when I walked in.

"Um-m-m . . . . Hey." I knew better than to wake them up. But I just couldn't stand it, them two being in a place I couldn't go.

"Hello, Sister Lena," Sao says. Bo sort of opened his eyes and looked at me like he knew I knew I would spoil something, but I did it anyway. Then he closed them again. Sao didn't notice. She wouldn't.

"Did you have a nice day at work?" She always asks that and waits for an answer, like it matters.

"It was alright." Like it would be different. I mean, like suddenly boxcutters and price tags would be glamorous and exciting. All of the sudden, I make a resolution to start studying my vocabulary words all over again. I need something to say besides "alright."

"That's good," she says. "I'm glad you're doing well there."

She means that. She really thinks it's progress that they trust me to run the registers when the lines get too long, or it's a sign that they trust me. She thinks setting mugs of glass too thin to microwave in straight lines means that I am a responsible person. Sao thinks wielding the price gun means that I am getting somewhere in the world.

I like her for that.

"Where's Cumberland?" Bo asks, without opening his eyes.

At first, I took Cumberland with me to work in the truck. He waited outside of the craft shop. After a while, Nola said he could come in and rest behind the register, on account of he was good for business. People go plumb crazy over seeing an animal where they didn't expect one. Like a cat on the White House lawn. Or how I drive through Grady Lee's Bar-B-Que and when the drive-through people see Cumberland, they go all to pieces. They call each other to the window and start talking to Cumberland in shrill, excited voices.

"Oh, a doggie," they squeal. "Can he have some Chicken Slivers? Sauce? There's no MSG." Then they feed Cumberland like he's a paying customer or like he'll tell all his dog friends.

"You'uns come back," they shout, waving. Cumberland is busy eating his barbeque. Same thing over at Dairy Holler. The teenagers wave and exclaim over Cumberland and give him a kiddie cone and cheeseburger patties. I guess seeing an animal kind of makes their day.

The way Nola figures it, Cumberland is good for an extra ten percent on every order. Customers get everything they want together, bring it up to the register, and there they see Cumberland. Him being the gentlemanly dog he is, he sits up and wags his tail so that they can see him and pet him and make a general big fuss over seeing a dog in the store. Then, when they look back to their purchases at the counter, Nola has set out beaded rings made by a little lady over in Big Cove, who has five girls and churns rings out by the hundred, and copies of the local paper, and *News from Indian Country*, *Whispering Wind*, *Indian Life*, and authentic Cherokee-made tom-toms. After visiting with Cumberland, the average buyer picks up at least one more item than they had planned on buying.

Cumberland walks in right then, hearing his name. He goes over to the recliner. He sets down there and wags his tail, waiting for somebody to pet him.

"I'd pet you, Cumberland, but I've been laying brick and my arms are tired," Bo says. His eyes are still closed, and I see the beginnings of gray in his brows. Then, Cumberland does something that if I had me a camera, I'd record and send over to one of those TV shows about real smart pets or something. He rises up and eases his head under Bo's hand. Bo scratches Cumberland's ears.

"You are so smart, Cumberland," Sao says. Cumberland sits down for a second. Then he walks right around that chair and sits under the part where you rest your feet. Like a picture of a family, if Norman Rockwell drew Cherokee bricklayers and their sweet wives and somebody else's dog.

I don't know why I keep on talking. I should just turn around and take a shower or something. But I feel shut out, like I can't leave well enough alone.

"Cumberland must remember you helping him."

Sao shrugs. "God helped him. I just like him."

"Well, I guess I'd like anyone who could do magic, too." As soon as I say that, I feel bad about it. I know Sao won't hold it against me and that makes it worse. Bo raises an eyebrow over his shut eyes. He caught that.

"Miracles." Sao says this gently, like she is reminding me of what fork to use or not to dig in my nose at the dinner table.

"Is there a difference? One that dogs can tell?" I feel like doing little mean things to people. I remind myself to change this.

Sao nods. "Definitely. Magic is lots of bells and whistles. Smoke and mirrors. And at the end of it all, whatever happens, you find yourself looking at the person who did it. They get all the credit and all of the applause. Miracles make you look ordinary, even foolish if God doesn't do what you ask Him to do. A miracle never looks like a miracle. It looks like a bag lunch and a hungry crowd or a funeral procession or a prison sentence—" Bo smiles at that one.

I cannot stand it. "Or a bloody dog in the drive."

Sao shifts, leans over, reaches under the footrest. She pats Cumberland—not pats exactly, but sort of puts her hand on him for a minute.

"Yes," she says, "sometimes a miracle looks like a bloody dog in the driveway."

"Could you do it again?"

"Do what again?"

"What you done for Cumberland. Could you do it again?"

"No. I mean, I don't know. Maybe. I mean, I didn't do it the first two times. God did. And the thing about God is that He can do anything He wants to, anyway He wants to do it. I kind of think that I was on active duty, and now I'm more like the reserves. Rescuing people isn't my line of duty anymore."

"Superman," Bo murmurs.

"Superman?" I ask. Nothing.

"Superman?" Sao asks and Bo answers her.

"Yeah, Baby. Superman. Superman had all these super-powers, but he gave them up to be with Lois Lane. One day, he's leaping tall buildings in a single bound, next he's getting beat up in barfights and sh . . . " he pauses, pats Sao on her hip, "stuff. He goes from having nothing to fear but kryptonite to having to look both ways before he crosses the street. Just having to cross the street is a comedown for Superman."

For a minute, I hope I can start a fight. I don't know what's gotten into me, but I speak my mind before I remember to be sorry.

"Was it worth it?"

Sao doesn't so much as blink before she answers. "Flying is overrated."

Bo reaches for her then, pulls her onto his chest. They both shut their eyes. Sao puts her hand on where Bo's heart should be, and he moans, long and low, from some-place deep in his big chest. Cumberland is snoring.

I think about flopping down on the sofa. I think about waking Cumberland up and taking him out on the porch with me. But instead, I walk into the kitchen, where Sao has fixed chicken and rice—rosy poyo I think she calls it—and some dumplings with pinto beans in them.

"You go ahead and eat," I hear Bo call out. "We're going to have a nap."

Right about then, I hear Sao laugh. An exclamation point—only it's at the beginning of a sentence made out of quiet and no words at all.

Make No Tarrying

Bo Notices Certain

"I don't like her." Bo Notices says this softly, into my collarbone.

"I'm not sure I do either," I confess.

Bo Notices widens his eyes. "Then what's she doing here for months?"

"I don't know. I don't have any idea. I think she's trying. I just can't see turning her away."

"I can."

I kiss Bo Notices' shoulder. "If you want her gone, then gone she is."

Bo stretches. "You're so nice." He means this.

"I mean it, Bo. You say you want her gone, then gone she is."

"You said that already."

Bo thinks for a minute. "Do you love me? A yes-or-no question. No roundabout answers."

He startles me. "Of course, I love you."

"Then trust me."

"I do."

Bo Notices sighs. "I know trash. I was trash. And that girl, she's trash, sure enough."

"Put her out, then. Or I will. Just say when."

"In a moment," Bo Notices whispers. "First things first."

What I Would

Sao Notices Noticing

I disobey my husband. I don't know why. Maybe I am afraid that if I send this girl away, she will take my father again from my mother. Maybe I have traces of saintly residue left on my soul, the leavings of spiritual pollen or frost. Maybe sainthood without the super powers is deadly. Ask Superman.

Maybe maybe is the problem. Maybe we are looking at Lena as maybe trouble, or maybe we did find somebody God can't really change. And the thing about maybe is that, most times, it doesn't get here. We worry about maybe this will happen, or maybe that will happen, but it doesn't, and we missed what is or was, worrying about maybe. Maybe we are wrong about this confused girl and her sweet little dog. Maybe I am wrong about me. Maybe I am making excuses.

If there is a reason why I don't ask Lena to leave, it's probably that I'm in it now. That's my new philosophy, fashioned from lectures and meddling. When my husband married me, there's no telling how many people went out of their way to let me know exactly how much and how hard and how long they would disapprove. I prayed about it and sat bolt upright in the bed, and said right out loud, "I'm in it now." That solved everything.

"I'm in it now," I told God. "Maybe all these people, Mamí, Papí, the Holiness elders are right, but I'm in it now. And right, wrong, or indifferent, I'm asking You to make it work."

And He did. At least for my husband and for me. Lena, I'm not quite sure. I think I let her stay because she's here now, and we're in it now, and maybe I think that if I leave it lay, things will turn out. But they won't. Things left to their own devices usually don't get better. Mountains erode, lottery winners go bankrupt. When children get quiet, that's the time to worry. I know this, but I don't act like I know. Every day, it gets harder to break Lena's plate.

Broken Pieces

Bo Notices Troubled

When I was in the service, we got leave. A buddy of mine wanted to check out this carnival. All of a sudden, a drunk came out of nowhere, begging for money. Here I was, outrunning my old life, and maybe I saw myself back before I put on the uniform. Maybe I saw my dad after he had a few too many. I don't know. All I know is I shook my head, told him no when he asked me. He put his hand on my arm as I passed.

"May you get what you want," he whispered.

It's that whisper I think of now. At the time, I called him crazy, went on to ride the ferris wheel and eat handfuls of cotton candy. Now I know I should've emptied my wallet, wrote an IOU, anything to keep those words from turning into a curse.

See, I've got what I want, the only thing I want. And she wants this girl, this white trash, ugly-duckling girl, to turn into some kind of Christian swan. If this girl was a man, I'd set him out in the road. But she isn't, and I haven't, and every time we set down to supper, I think what my wife wants might cost me.

The Necks of Kings

Lena Allen Mays Living

One thing I'll say for Bo Notices, he's got himself a good job with the tribe. Works construction. He made foreman, so he gets an hour for lunch. Drives ten minutes here, stays thirty, and heads back to the site. Bo Notices tells Sao it makes his day better if he comes home just to look at her. Fridays, he brings his check right home and puts it in her lap. She always gives it back to him. Then she does something that'd make any man go back to work on Monday.

She thanks him.

Really. She says, "Thank you, Bo." But it ain't what she says, it's the way she says it. I mean, everybody says that about words, and people say thank you a thousand times in a day, but when Sao says it, it's different. I can't exactly say how, except if I could bottle it and sell it, nobody would ever get divorced again. I guess it's that she means it, really means it, like she's grateful that Bo gets up at dawn, lifts brick after brick, and comes home every day. Like she appreciates that after doing all that, he'd bring home his pay and take care of her. I mean, a body might think I'm making too much out of it, until they see Bo Notices.

If somebody could grow another foot in a minute, Bo'd be doing it. The minute she says thank you and hands that check back to him, it's like the whole room just fills up. Then, they get in the Jeep and drive into town to deposit the check at the credit union and go over to Sylva or even Asheville to eat. They never invite me. Not that they should. But I don't know—I wish they would or that I had somebody who would.

Now, I know that ain't right, as good and hospitable as the Notices have been to me. But Bo never even notices me—no pun intended—and it's like the only thing he can see is Sao. I don't know if he's even said so much more than "boo" to me since I got here. He is nice to Cumberland, though. The other morning, Bo made breakfast in bed for Sao, and he cooked up two pieces of bacon for Cumberland.

Cumberland—now that's somebody else smitten with Sao, sure enough. I mean, he follows her from room to room and barks every so often so she'll stop and pet his head. Just let her sit down for a second and Cumberland's right there. He puts his head on her feet and goes to sleep.

Thursday, I got back early from my other job at the candle shop. There's this little shop in downtown, if you can say this town has a downtown, and Nola's brother-in-law owns it. It sells candles, mostly, and made-in-Taiwan souvenirs. It's a hoot what people will buy. Plaster-of-Paris Indian heads and black velvet paintings of wolves howling at the moon. All the Indian maidens on the greeting cards are half dressed, and all the men are put-near naked and carrying bows and arrows. That's funny, since most of the real Indians you see are wearing jeans and T-shirts.

That's one thing I thought would be different. You never can tell about people, but I kindly thought they'd be glad to see me. Not sure why, but I thought maybe they'd recognize me or welcome me or something. I guess that's foolish, since Mama was from Oklahoma, but I figured Cherokee there, Cherokee here. One day I went to church with Bo and Sao, and some girl named Sally rolled her eyes at me and said, "Are you enrolled?"

"No," I told her, "I don't go to school at this time."

She just sniggered and walked off. Bo told me not to mind her. Maybe I shouldn't, but I think Sao should. Sally seems to be a little sweet on Bo.

Most of the Indians just sort of pass me by. Except for the men, who holler at me out of truck windows, while I pump my gas. They didn't know me before, so I guess it may take a while for them to see how much I changed.

If the Indians ignore me, the tourists sure don't. At first, they seem a little disappointed to find what looks like a white girl working behind the counter of the candle shop. I don't know why, seeing as that's what they'd see in the mall, but the malls is what people come here to get away from. Looks like they expect different from an Indian candle shop.

First thing they usually ask, after they put their faces back together from not seeing any "real" Indians, is "Where are the tipis?"

I tell them that Cherokee didn't ever live in tipis—that was way out West. I use my most knowledgeable voice to say this, and they are obviously impressed. Next, they usually ask me if I am an Indian, and I point to Mama's birth certificate, which I had copied at the grocery and taped on the wall behind the register. Customers cheer up then and are glad to be talking to a "real" Indian. A lot of times, moms call their kids over and tell them to look at me and see a real live Cherokee Indian. Other times, especially with the old couples, they ask all day of questions, checking up on information that they got out of history books or off the history shows. One time a lady from South Carolina just out and out apologized.

She stood at the register and started crying. I thought maybe she had a condition or needed a doctor. When I asked her who I could call—I didn't know, because only Indians can use the hospital here—she grabbed onto my hand. She squalled until big drops of water and salt and stuff it would be rude to name splashed onto the glass counter where we keep the Navajo turquoise jewelry and essential oils.

"Please forgive me," she bawled. "I am so sorry."

Her words shocked me. I thought maybe I knew her in my old life, but she looked too old for somebody I used to get drunk with. And too rich to be one of Daddy's women. Her hair was set, like she had been to the beauty parlor. And her teeth. That's one way you can tell somebody comes from quality. Their teeth are all in their head, straight, no spots. Her lipstick was this pale shade of pink that looks like lips, that classy ladies tend to wear.

"What did you do?" I looked around for a napkin, a tissue, something. Only a piece of tissue paper for wrapping jewelry. I considered a square of cotton from the bottom of a jewelry box. The lady opened her pocketbook, the kind with handles and cloth covers that button to close, and pulled out a handkerchief with tiny irises stitched on it. Real ladies never have to dig through their pocketbooks.

"Oh, all of it. I mean slavery, reservations, the Trail of Tears, Jim Crow. I just feel so bad about it. I mean, my grandaddy used to *lynch* people. They'd string them up and leave them hanging from trees for the flies and their families to find."

This is terrible, but I don't see how it means me. Mrs. Dukes and her fried chicken crossed my mind, and I hoped

Mr. Dukes is doing alright. I forgot to ask them to pray for me, I think, but maybe they will anyway.

"Well, you didn't do it."

She shook her roller-set hair. "Oh, I as good as did. Because of what we—my people—did to you all, to your people, I inherited acres of land and plenty of money, and we've always had, well, you know, help." She mentioned "help" in a low whisper, like she was sharing nuclear secrets with me or something. I couldn't see why she needed charity if she had all that land and money, but I kept that to myself.

"Well, you didn't do it." I felt like a stuck record. I remembered records and all of the sudden, I felt very old. Marthal's little bitty niece came with her one time to see about us and ran right over to Mama's old RCA. She picked up one of Mama's records and said, right out, "What's this big old CD?" I felt about like the people on the ark, like there was a whole world that happened before and washed away before I could tell this toddler about it.

"Yes, but I reaped the benefits. Judge Clay and I— Judge Clay is my husband—were finishing our Sunday dinner—Othelda makes the best custard pies!—and all of a sudden, it dawned on me. Our savings account, our cruise after Christmas, our summer place, all were made possible by these terrible wrongs. Well, I felt so very awful that I could only eat one slice of custard pie. And Othelda worked on that dinner all day. Missed church even. One slice! Judge Clay asked me what was the matter, and I told him I just couldn't bear the fact that I was so rich and so successful on account of the pain of other people. He told me some famous historian said that every great culture grows on the bones of another. Still, it was unbearable."

"Yeah, but what are you going to do about it now?"

She put the hand with the handkerchief over my hand, which was already held in hers. Sort of a hand sandwich.

"That's why I'm here, Sweetie. I aim to apologize to as many In—Native American people as I possibly can. I went to the Gullah Islands last spring and I spent all day telling the Col—African American people how sorry I am. Next I went to Greenville and went right downtown and apologized to as many people as would let me. I'm here this weekend, and next weekend, I aim to ride over and make amends to the Lumbee and the Saponi. I thought, in between, I might find some Melungeons. I'm not sure if I've hurt them in any way or not, but better safe than sorry."She sniffles.

"Does your husband mind you doing this?"

"Why no, Dear, he gives me money each month for the trips. He saw I was carrying on so, and everything seemed so very bad that he did everything in his power to help me. He even sent Othelda with me down to Greenville."

My daddy had a word for people like this. He'd say this lady was a loon, but I'm not so sure. She seems to mean every word she's saying.

"So," she says, tears streaming from reddened eyes. "Will you please forgive me?"

I'm not so sure I'm in any position to forgive anybody. But if it will make her happy, I can try.

"Sure," I say, adding as much cheerfulness as I can.

Her eyes dry up immediately. "Thank you," she replies, "Now, how much do I owe you?"

She chatters about sandpaintings while I ring her up. She explains how the candles with the longest-lasting wicks are wider, not taller, when I hand her her change.

"Goodbye," she says. She walks out of the shop's front door and right into a local boy with dark skin and a ponytail. The tears, and I suppose the apologies, start all over again.

When I came in from working, Cumberland was sitting right up on the sofa with his head on Sao's belly. He was sound asleep. Sao was reading a book about having a good Christian marriage and all that. I smell lemon and pine and the smells like when the good mom on TV's been cleaning.

"Cumberland," I said, "get off that sofa."

Cumberland just opened one eye before he went back to sleep.

"I'm sorry, Sao," I said, "he'll make your sofa dirty."

Sao smiles at me. "I gave him a bath this morning."

The news startles me. I've never known Cumberland to like bathwater. "How'd you get him to stay in it?" I can't help myself but ask.

"I put buttermilk in the water," Sao explains. "He was a gentleman."

"Oh," I say, wondering what buttermilk had to do with my dog acting right in water.

I stand there for a moment. "Most people don't like dogs on their sofa."

Sao sets her book down next to her. "There's plenty of room if you want to join us."

I haven't had a bath. I smell like the dumpster behind the candle shop. "Maybe later," I say. "I think I'd best get in the shower first." I head up the stairs, hoping that Cumberland will follow. He keeps on sleeping and Sao goes back to reading.

Anyhow, Bo and Sao have been real nice about letting me stay here. Not even charging me rent or nothing for the months we've been here.

"Wait until you get on your feet," Sao told me, the first time I brought it up. That's good, too, since my job is just part-time, and I have to feed me and Cumberland, plus put gas in the truck.

I didn't come with nothing but a few of Mama's old dresses, my jeans, and my underwear. A few days afterward, Sao went to the Baptist Ladies' Thrift Store and came home with two skirts, four shirts, and a new pair of penny loafers.

"How much I owe you?" I asked her. I never had anybody go out of their way like this before.

Sao shook her head. "It's on us. We want you to have a good start here." Then she reached in her pocket and handed me two of the newest pennies I ever did see. Shining like they was minted last year. They were.

"For your shoes," Sao said. I about bawled right then and there.

One morning, I ask Sao how old she is. It don't even occur to me that I might be rude.

"Thirty," Sao says.

My mouth falls open. "Thirty!"

"Thirty," she replies.

"I'm sorry," I tell her, "I didn't mean to make you out a liar. And you should know how old you are, after all. It's just you don't look thirty."

Sao smiles. "Holiness living. You don't burn up your lungs or wrinkle your skin smoking. Don't squint at movie screens or tear up your liver drinking. Stay home all the time, and you're pretty much safe from crime. Frostbite and sunburn can't get under long sleeves or in prayer meetings. Anything else, you can pretty much rebuke."

Sao is as serious as she can be. Real, they'd say back home. I think that's why her husband can't see nothing but her. I get the impression that Bo Notices has had to work for every bit of credit he gets in these parts. I can tell without him telling that Bo Notices used to be mean—trouble even. But Sao believes in him. That changed his whole life.

That's why he wants to be around Sao so much. Partly because she builds him up and partly because he doesn't have anybody else. Whether Sao knows it or not, that's how you do it. Get somebody grateful. It's like a dog-pound dog. See, Cumberland, he won't eat nothing he don't like. I picked up some dog food in the One-Dollar Store and put it right back down. Cumberland won't eat anything cheap like that. He's used to something. But a dog-pound dog, he's grateful for anything you give him. And he sure won't leave you. I used to throw anything Daddy burned out in the backyard back home. Sure enough, it wouldn't be long before mutts came and ate it up. Cumberland, it got to be jack mackerel or nothing.

So Sao did right getting a man that's grateful. Funny thing is, she's grateful too. I don't understand that, when she's so pretty and she can get God to make it rain. But she is grateful. Maybe she was just as set back in her old life as Bo was in his. Back in Kentucky, Sao was somebody everybody talked about but nobody was brave enough to talk to. Maybe that's it right there. Maybe once you've talked to somebody like that, you don't need anybody else. Maybe that's why Bo can only see Sao. Maybe that's why he will never see me.

What We Lost

Sao Notices Cautioned

When things are going astray, I say,
I see spiders.
In the sink, in the corners,
Mourners,
Warning the transgression of law,
good sense, and commandments,
One too many flaws.
I look both ways
And pray
Until atonement is made.

I know what you mean,
Bo tells me.
When I'm wrong, I see clowns.
Yeah, clowns.
It's some kind of funny that hides behind cork,
Powders doubt behind greasepaint and ashes.
All to convince us that his laugh is
Not at all cursing us under color clashes.
Yellow for smallpox,
Blue for the veins,
He knows he will open with shotguns and pain.

Green for the land that was stolen away.
Red,
By now, red should be self-explanatory.

I tell Abuelita.
Mi corazón, she says,
Thank Jesus for every spider you see.
It's the ones you don't that should cause you worry.
Those are the ones that know how to spin crafty,
To mock dust and down at the edge of a pillow,
To wait in the eyelet, the change of a case.
Those are the ones, when they need to, choose,
To hide in the round at the heel of a shoe.
Those are the ones who bite by surprise.
Siphon blood, leave bile of rot and lies.
When you see them, you can still win the war.

This morning, before trouble shows itself at our door,
I see spiders.
Spiders, spiders everywhere.

The Tenth Commandment

Lena Allen Mays Coveting

If I live to be a hundred, I don't think I'll know why I do what I do. I walk into Bo and Sao's living room, and there is Bo Notices, all stretched out on the sofa. His hair is all spread out over the throw pillow. He snores, dead to the world. People like that who can sleep through anything, even daylight, amaze me.

Bo Notices has his shirt off. Every muscle shows under sweat. But that don't excuse what I do next. I shut the front door behind me and kneel beside the couch. This is all I want at first, I swear, to kiss the muscle right above his navel. Which I do, lightly. I taste salt and sweat, and I kiss him again right below. My fingers slide loose the button of his jeans. I start to tug on his zipper before he sits up.

Somebody smacks me. Hard. I feel like a cartoon character, with stars and bells and whistles going off around my head. Sao has hold of my ponytail and drags me by it out of the front door. Then she pushes me off the porch. The door locks behind me.

I sit on the grass for a moment. Stunned. I pull my keys out of my pocket. Then, I drive away. Fast. But like Sao says, I take myself with me.

The Sea of the Priests

Sister Jane Washing

Look at what passes for love around here. A Holiness handshake—a firm grip with a folded five-dollar bill passed from palm to palm. Hugs with back-patting, like you'd burp a baby. And the words, "I love you," hollow and shrill, with no more meaning behind them than reading the phone book out loud.

I married my husband for what I thought was love. You've heard me talk about the way I was hurt, almost torn in two by the GoingBack boy when I was just a girl. It's my testimony, on Christian television and in crusades. The audience most often shouts when I tell about how God restored my beauty and my virtue in the same day. Then I tell them how, at that moment, I knew that I would do anything I could do for God, I loved Him that much.

The part I don't tell, leastways not in crusades, is how I mixed up love for God with doing things for God. I told God I'd do anything He told me to do, and I meant it so much that I got myself confused. When my husband rode into town, preaching hellfire and brimstone, pointed right at me and said it was God's will for me to be his wife, I didn't have any better sense than to believe it. And I wouldn't say a word against my husband on account of he's a preacher and a good man of God, but if I had it to do over, I'd try the spirits.

Mainly on account of me never having a baby. Every time somebody quotes that Scripture about God giving us the desires of our hearts, I think, well, why not for me. My husband told me wait, wait, until he finally came right out and said he'd hate to be at Judgment Day and find out he could have gotten more souls saved if we hadn't had our own home and family to tie us down.

The news nearly killed me, that's for sure. Just choked the wind right out of my airway. I remember gasping when I got hurt, the way my mind went wild with the need for air. My hands grasped at my husband's ankles as I fell to the floor, and I heard myself begging, crying out for just one, only one. I could put her in a basket and she wouldn't be no trouble. Please. But my husband said that was the end of it; he had spoken. He never laid down in the same bed with me again.

Frankly, it's hard to argue with that kind of devotion. And I know better than to fuss back at my husband, especially since he works for God. Questioning God was out of the question. There were always babies in the healing lines, and I often hoped that God would move on somebody to let me keep one.

As many people who come out, you'd think we were loved. But we aren't. We're just necessary. The halt, the lame, the blind, the afflicted, they just want to get better. The drunkard, the harlot, and the sinner, they just want to be free. All of them willing to chew and swallow the words we offer, get their miracle, then go on home.

We come out to Cherokee, North Carolina, quite a bit, on account of we're Western Cherokee. It's like coming home really, since we all came from here, before we took a long walk West during the Trail of Tears. It's said that some of the old people took one look at Oklahoma's flat land and died. No trees, no mountains, no place to look up to. Just dry and dusty, as far as the eye could see.

My husband likes it here. He says there are plenty of souls to save and church people to upgrade. All the Holiness folks laugh when he says this. This land is beautiful. I get afraid when I stay too long. There are so many places where I could hide.

Tonight, we have a meeting at the Ceremonial Grounds. Every service is about the same, to start with. I sing, and then I testify for the Lord. That's one thing: I don't bite my tongue when it comes to talking about what God has done. After that, my husband comes out with the message.

Then there's the healing line. That's where God shows up and shows out. I mean, I've seen Him do about everything. One time a little lady's left leg grew until it matched her right one, right there. A teenage girl spit up a cancer. It looked just like a man-o-war jellyfish, with tentacles and everything. Somebody spilled sawdust over it, and it moved like it was swimming until it died. One time a man brought a woman in on a stretcher. They were on the way to the hospital in an ambulance when they passed our tent. We still had that big tent at that time, seated hundreds in metal folding chairs. I'll tell you one thing, my husband never took to any prejudice either. First in, first row, regardless of what color you were. This man's wife was hemorrhaging and they couldn't stop the blood. Right then, I shouted out Ezekiel 16:6, "And when I passed by thee, and saw thee polluted in thine own blood, I said unto thee when thou wast in thy blood. Live." And God stopped it, just like that.

That little woman still sends me cards at Christmas. Each one has a ten-dollar bill. "FOR YOU," she writes in big, capital letters. "FOR YOUR USE ONLY, PLEASE." She signs each one, "Love, Sister Gussie." Scrawled, looping letters, like maybe her hands hurt. I pray over the letters, in case she has arthritis. She never does say. I put the money in an account for someday. My husband is a lot older than I am. I think that if Jesus tarries, I'll take that money and put a house on my family's land.

It's funny how God chooses whom He chooses. After my healing, I discovered that I could pray for people and they would get better. Just like that. Even hard cases. In the beginning, my husband would drive me over to the Methodist Hospital. We'd walk up and down the corridors, and I'd stop in and pray for people. Anybody I put my hands on got a miracle.

Except me. I prayed and prayed for a baby. Instead, our ministry grew. My husband got the tent from a traveling evangelist, Brother Leonard, over in Rankin Hill, Kentucky. We went on the road and I sang and my husband did the preaching. Now we hold our meetings in auditoriums. Too much liability with a tent. A strong wind can land you in a load of lawsuits. Civic centers are safer. Insurance comes with the building.

Over the years, I've laid my hands on little girls, girls I thought might replace me someday. I used to think that if I could just pass on this anointing, God might let me go free to be a wife and mother. Maybe my husband would see me as a regular woman, one that needs to knit booties and tuck somebody in at night. I'd do my best to pass the power along, make sure that someone else could do what I could, most of all so I'd no longer have to do it.

I repented of that, though. I consider the treasures laid up for us in Heaven and I try to be content. Most of the time, I am. As long as I don't sit too still, think too much, or for too long.

Tonight I open the service with *I Need Thee*. It's right then that I see her. She's back tonight. A girl with long hair and smoker's teeth. She staggers into the back of the meeting hall like she's running from something. She flops into a chair and puts her head in her hands. I can almost not listen to the message for watching God deal with her. When we make the altar call, invite the lost and the hurting, the confused and the sick to come forward for prayer, I watch her. First, she holds onto the chair in front of her. She gets up and heads for the door. The first night, she ran out. Same thing on the second. This night, she goes for the door. Her hands reach out to push it open before she turns around and runs up the aisle.

"I've ruined everything," she cries out over the organ music. "Everything!"

"That's what God's for," I assure her, "to fix what we've broken."

"You don't understand," she hollers. "You don't know what I've done."

"I'm not so sure I need to know."

At that point, she throws her arms around me and sobs. I hold her in my arms. "Whatever it is, it's not so terrible that it can't at least be talked about."

And that's what we do after the service. We talk for an hour. I ask her how she came to be in these mountains in North Carolina, on this reservation.

"Whenever I first got back in church, I found this." I recognize Daddy in the photograph she shows me. He is so handsome that tears come to my eyes. The second photo makes me forget to remember to breathe. I see my sisters—Georgia, Carolina, Indiana, and myself. I was Tenessee Jane then. I had forgotten I was that beautiful. I cannot believe we were ever that young.

"That's my mama," the girl explains, pointing.

I know. I remember.

She hands me a folded piece of card stock. A birth certificate. Georgia StandsStraight.

I was a StandsStraight once.

"I found out we are Indian—Cherokee Indian—so I figured I'd come here. I don't know what exactly I thought I'd find."

"But your mama was born in Oklahoma," I note.

She nods. "I know," she agrees, "but me and Cumberland only had enough money to get down here to North Carolina."

"Who's Cumberland?"

"My dog. He's back at the house, where I . . . where I done what I did." Her face folds as if she is about to cry again.

"That's what is to be done," my voice sounds calmer, stronger than I feel. "You need to go back to them and ask their forgiveness."

"What if they hate me?"

"They might. That's between them and God. Your job is to put things as close to right as you can."

"Then what?"

I sigh. "I'm not so sure that's your concern. God's got to have something to do."

"What if they tell me I have to leave?"

"We can always use help with our next crusade. We're heading back to Oklahoma in a few days. You could ride with us and usher or something. Can you sing?"

"Not so you'd want to hear it."

"You don't know what you can do if God gets in it."

"Will God help me apologize?"

"Ask Him and I'm sure He will."

As I watch my older sister's daughter walk away, my lower lip jumps, like a tic, only it stops. If she comes back to me, I will take her to Oklahoma, show her to my mother, to her grandfather, and her Aunt Carolina. I almost stop her, call her back to tell her who she is. Something bites my lip again. I let God decide if she needs to know.

Desire of the Nations

Sister Tennessee Jane Satisfied

We leave undone,
What we should have done,
Laundry,
Beadwork,
The weaving of thread,
The singing of church songs,
The baking of bread,
                         Instead
We press,
Find the hem of His garment,
And
Pull.

Flaming Sword

Bo and Sao Notices Restored

My wife rolls her eyes. "That sounds like a *heathen* story."
She winks at me. I go all to pieces. It's funny about my
wife and me. Everything about her is alright with me.
More than alright. I mean the way she laughs, what she
says, it's just right. Like whenever we first got married,
she was worried about how to love me on account of me
being, well, the way I used to live before we got together.
But that's as good as it can be.

I mean, if anybody'd ever told me I could love anybody more than myself, I might've called them a few
things I don't care to mention. But that's how it is for me
and my wife. She's my heart. I mean that. I mean, I would
never have touched that trash, not for a thousand pieces
of silver. I know my wife knows that, but she's been so
quiet. She doesn't turn me away, but she doesn't turn
toward me, either. Not so quick as before.

So Friday night—the Friday night three days after—I
wake my wife.

"Honey," I ask her, "will you let me take you somewhere?"

Now, I got me a good woman when I married my wife.
Most women today, they'd look at you like you had gone

plumb foolish, wanting to go somewhere in the middle of the night. But my wife sits up without a word. She goes to the closet and pulls on the dress I bought her last payday. Denim, without sleeves. Buttons down the front, from the collar to the bottom. I pull on my jeans and a T-shirt.

"We'll take my bike," I tell my wife. She puts on a pair of leggings.

By the time we get to Soco Strawberry Farm, my skin is walking. I know how my wife loves to eat strawberries. She says her mother ate just about nothing next to strawberry pie when she was carrying her. I try to bring her good berries, in season, as often as I can. She'll smile at me and say, "Fresh strawberries!"

Like I'd bring her any other kind. Then I say, "They were just living," and she offers me the first bite. I never cared too much for strawberries, but I do now.

That's one of the things I like best about my wife. How we have these ways, these words to talk to each other. They don't mean anything but to us. Such as when I say "they were just living," back to her. Or when she says, "Heathen," the way Sally Rideout used to. I was watching a documentary one time that said one of the ways a culture qualifies to be a culture is that it has its own ways of communicating. I'm not sure we are a culture, but we sure make a good little family.

"Ta-dah! Here we are!" I know how my wife thinks, so I say, right fast, "No, it is *not* illegal. Bennis, the owner, is my daddy's first cousin. Here, my dear, is your basket." I hand her an IGA bag. I expect her to laugh, but she doesn't.

I walk over to the strawberries and start picking. My hands are shaking. My wife hesitates for a moment before she starts picking the berries. I'll say this, I've never been scared of much of anything in my life. Until now. I watch my wife under the full moon, and all I want is for her to stop and say, "Bo, it's alright. It's not no different than it's ever been." But she doesn't.

"Once upon a time, there were only two people in the whole world. First Man and First Woman."

My wife stops to listen. I get braver. I swallow hard, so she won't hear that I wasn't this steady a minute ago.

"Well, First Man and First Woman had a quarrel over something and First Woman left. Obviously, this didn't look too good for the human race, so God had to do something." I swallow hard. Again. "So He couldn't let First Woman get too far away from her husband. So he put a strawberry plant right there. Ripe, red berries. First Woman never had seen anything quite like that before, so she stopped running off long enough to try it out. But God's so smart, He only had four berries. Each one sweeter than the last. When First Woman finished them, she kept walking. By that time, First Man had set out after her."

My wife smiles at me. Not like usual, but enough to keep me going.

"Well, it was going to take him a minute to catch up. So God put plant after plant in First Woman's path. By the time she stopped and ate enough times, First Man had time to catch up."

"What'd he do then?" I am so glad to hear my wife's voice that I nearly shout.

"Well," I tell her, "I'm not all the way sure about that part of the story. But whatever it was, it must have worked, because the rest of us are here."

That's when my wife rolls her eyes. "That sounds like a *heathen* story," she says, winking at me. I'm good to go right there. She turns back to picking berries.

I'll do anything to keep her talking to me. "Tell me a better one then."

She shrugs. "I'll try, but you're the storyteller. I'd rather hear you."

"Then see how you like this one," I say. "Once upon a time, not as long ago as Noah or the Flood, there was a man. A man whose daddy drank and whose mama did, too. And when they drank, they took turns beating on that man—only he was a boy then. And that boy grew up to be a man. Not a special man, but a regular man. Only he drank, too, and more besides. And just when he thought that he couldn't get any worse and couldn't get any better, he met God. And since God couldn't be there in person to put His arms around that man or sit across the dinner table from him or ride on the back of his Harley, He sent him a wife to stand in for Him."

My eyes water. I'm so scared inside, from a place I can't name. "Sao, I'm sorry. I wouldn't have . . . . I mean, never. The only woman I ever wanted is you. Even when I didn't know you, even when there were other women before I met you, I wanted you. That girl, I wouldn't have . . . I mean . . . . Please, Sao."

My wife turns to face me. Her eyes are wet. She drops her bag and comes toward me. I feel her arms around me. I'm shaking.

"No, no," she whispers in my ear. "I'm not angry with you. I'm angry with *me*. You didn't do anything wrong. I'm just so sorry I didn't listen to you, that I let that happen to you . . . to us. Please, forgive me."

"Please don't leave me, Sao." That comes out, between sobs.

"Leave you?" My wife pulls away to look into my eyes. "Where would I go? I can't live without my heart." She smiles at me, a real smile this time. I press her against me, so hard I can feel every button on that denim dress.

She holds onto me for I don't know how long. Somewhere in that field, under the moon, I cry everything out. The years I spent drunk, the days I wasted hiding out from school, all those times I laid down with any woman but Sao. My wife lets me cry.

"Do you want to hear a story?" She asks, wiping my eyes with the hem of her dress.

I nod.

"Once upon a time, there was a man all alone in a garden. God said that wasn't good, so He made a woman just perfect for him. And the man and the woman made mistakes—sinned, really—and got evicted. No more peace, no more prosperity, no more long walks with God in the cool of the day. But God left them love, so they could remember what it was like to be loved by Him."

"That's a good story," I tell my wife, squeezing her close to me.

My wife squeezes back. "So is ours," she answers.

"I hope it stays good."

"It gets better."

"How?"

My wife whispers into my ear. I holler out, loud as I can, shouting over strawberry fields and toward the moon, telling God I knew I heard Him when He said we made ourselves a son.

Ordinary Time

Lena Allen Mays Repenting

If I could, I would go inside and tell them I am sorry. I would tell them I know better now, and I think of taking their goodness for granted and it hurts and makes me tired all at the same time.

My suitcase is waiting for me outside. Sao comes to the door.

"Sao," my throat feels tight inside, "I'm sorry."

"It took us so very long to be happy," she says. "We can't take the risk of anybody harming that. But I forgive you."

"I understand," I answer. And I do.

Sao pushes Cumberland out of the door. I say pushes, but shoves really. I pick Cumberland up and put him in the truck. He does not want to go. All of the sudden, I know that he shouldn't. He should stay here, where the people are happy. It's like a movie—the happy couple and their dog. If they ever have a baby, Cumberland can be the baby's dog.

"I love you, Cumberland," I tell my dog. "More than I ever loved anything or anybody. And you're welcome to come along with me. But I understand if you'd rather stay put and be their dog. They need somebody to watch out for them." I get out of the truck and put Cumberland on the ground.

Cumberland tilts his head for a minute. Without so much as a goodbye, Cumberland heads to the front door. He barks once, twice, and Sao opens the door. Cumberland's tail wags the whole back end of his body. Cumberland walks right in, like he lives there. Which he does now.

I pull out of the drive and head down the road. My eyes sting. I miss Cumberland, but I know I am doing right, leaving him there.

Sister Jane said they were heading for Oklahoma. Six weeks of revival and healing crusades. Maybe I could help out after all. Maybe see about finding Jack StandsStraight and if there's any left out of his girls. Most of all, I might could do something right about love.

The Worship of Angels

Bo and Sao Notices Rejoicing

What matters most is the weight of the heart,
The measure of fire,
The mind of God,
First, all and final, how we are made.

What matters most is the use of the heart,
The coming of children,
The gold standard of bread,
Day-in-day-out, how lives are made.

What matters at last is the joining of hearts,
The glimpses of Eden,
That make us miss Heaven,
How, in one another, we find it again.

Acknowledgments

"Angelphilia," "The Boiling Point of Conquest," "The Boundary of Moab," "Cast Salt," "Desire of the Nations," "What We Lost," and "The Worship of Angels" appear on Dawn Karima Pettigrew's spoken-word CD, *The Worship of Angels*. Cherokee, North Carolina: Wadulisi, 2005.

"A Bed in Hell" *Coloring Book: An Electic Anthology of Fiction and Poetry by Multicultural Writers*, Boice Terrel-Allen, editor, Pittsburgh, Penn.: Rattlecat Press, 2004.

"The Pursuit of Darkness" appeared as "Atasdi: Fish Story" in *Through the Eye of the Deer: An Anthology of Native American Women Writers*, Carolyn Dunn Anderson and Carol Comfort, editors, San Francisco: Aunt Lute Books, 1999; and in *The Year's Best Fantasy and Horror: Fourteenth Annual Collection*, Ellen Datlow and Terri Windling, editors, New York: St. Martin's Press, 2001.

"The Boiling Point of Conquest" in *Red Ink* 9, no. 1 (2000): 69.

"The Marriage of Saints" in *Glimmer Train Press, Inc.* 43 (2002): 119–134.

"Shewbread" appeared in slightly different form as "Manna Raptured" in *Femspec* 2, no. 2 (2001): 92–94.